"Marry me,"

He continued. "I'll take care of you and your baby and get control of the firm I've worked hard to build up over the last decade. Do we have a deal?"

Lindsay picked up the papers once more and reread them. It was a deal made in heaven for her. She would have the security she lacked and the means to spend time with her precious baby when it was born. And somehow it seemed justified, because the family that had caused her husband's death would now be in the family supporting her and her baby.

At least temporarily. Until Luke wanted his freedom.

She took a deep breath. "I guess we have a deal, Luke. I'll marry you whenever you say."

What happens when you suddenly discover your happy
twosome is about to be turned into a...*family*?

Do you panic?
Do you laugh?
Do you cry?
Or...do you get married?

The answer is all of the above—and plenty more!

Share the laughter and the tears as these unsuspecting
couples are plunged into parenthood! Whether it's a baby
on the way, or the creation of a brand-new instant family,
these men and women have no choice but to be

When parenthood takes you by surprise!

Look out in June 2001 for
Twins Included!
by Grace Green
#3658

TEMPORARY FATHER
Barbara McMahon

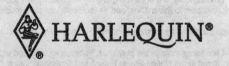

TORONTO • NEW YORK • LONDON
AMSTERDAM • PARIS • SYDNEY • HAMBURG
STOCKHOLM • ATHENS • TOKYO • MILAN • MADRID
PRAGUE • WARSAW • BUDAPEST • AUCKLAND

ISBN 0-373-03649-3

TEMPORARY FATHER

First North American Publication 2001.

CHAPTER ONE

LINDSAY Donovan sat at a table in the back of the café, her feet propped on the chair opposite her. Resting her cheek on one hand, she leafed through the notebook, trying to remember the pertinent points that she thought would be on tomorrow's exam. The garish overhead fluorescent lights illuminated the pages, bright as sunshine. The café was quiet except for the noise Jack made cleaning the grill in the kitchen. She and the crusty old bachelor had worked the evening shift together for more than six months, establishing a closeness that was not common among coworkers. Soon he'd walk her to the bus. They'd talk over their day and part. She was fond of the old man and knew he looked on her almost as a daughter.

When the outside door opened and a stranger entered, Lindsay glanced up, flicking a quick look at the huge clock that hung over the kitchen pass-through. It was almost midnight. Sighing softly, she rose awkwardly, hoping the customer didn't want a full meal. Ten minutes from closing was not the time to demand full service. Usually the last couple of hours were quiet. She hoped the customer would grab a quick cup of coffee then leave.

The man was tall, dark and in a tearing temper unless she missed her guess. Warily watching him as she moved to the counter, Lindsay eased her bulk behind it just as he took one of the stools. At least with counter service, she didn't have to carry a heavy tray. Eying his clothing, she wondered what he was doing at the café. It catered more to the working class than a man in a tux. Raising her gaze to his face, she frowned. There was a hint of familiarity in his features. Did she know him? He was not one of the

5

regular customers of the café. Yet there was definitely
something....

"Can I help you?" she asked. Despite her fatigue, her
discomfort, she suddenly wished she had combed her hair
and refreshed her lipstick. Interest piqued as she stared at
him—every woman's dream date. At least he would be if
he smiled. Instead, a dangerous air hovered around him. He
glanced at her for a second, anger shimmering in his eyes.
Lindsay was instantly glad she wasn't the cause of his anger.

The Friendly Corner Café was located on the fringes of
Sydney's docks. Its regular clientele didn't wear tuxedos,
nor expensive gold watches. Curious, Lindsay wondered
who he was and why he'd arrived so late at an out-of-the-
way café. What was he doing in this part of town dressed
as he was?

Suddenly her mind remembered. Summers at the beach
when she'd been a budding teenager. Before her parents'
death. Young and feeling full of herself, she'd flirted with
the older boys. And Luke Winters had been the one who
had caught her eye. Only a few years older than she, he'd
been her ideal romantic interest when she turned fourteen.
Slowly she smiled.

"Do I have time for a cup of coffee?" he asked, his eyes
scanning her, dismissing her as he glanced around the deserted diner.

"We close at midnight," she said, already reaching for
a cup and saucer. It pricked, that casual dismissal. Obviously she'd changed in the intervening years. But he could
have at least paused a moment as if trying to remember her.
Didn't he recognize her at all?

"I meant before you deliver," he said sardonically, his
gaze centered on her waist.

Lindsay straightened and glared at him. Old crush or not,
he had no right to be so scathing. "The baby is not due
for another couple of weeks. Plenty of time for you to have
a cup of coffee and get out."

He smiled maliciously, narrowing his dark eyes. "Not very customer-oriented, are you?"

"Not at eleven-fifty at night." She slammed down the saucer, relieved to note that the coffee didn't spill. She knew he'd make some snide comment if it had.

"Not bad," he said after taking a sip of the hot brew.

"I made it fresh just a little while ago. Do you want anything else? A piece of pie to go with it, or a sandwich?" Her response was rote, but her curiosity rose. Fascinated, she watched as he sipped the hot beverage. He'd aged, of course. But done it so well. What was he doing now? He'd been a bit of a rebel as a teenager. His family had had money, and he'd flaunted his contempt for the old order of things, coming to the beach in defiance of his mother's edicts, associating with the locals instead of the moneyed crowd. Did he still defy authority?

His snowy white shirt stood in stark contrast to his elegant tuxedo. Obviously made for him alone, it fit like a tailored dream. A dark overcoat was casually tossed over his broad shoulders. Apparently the damp coolness of the late spring night didn't faze him. His dark hair and almost black eyes made him seem a creature of the night. When he fixed his gaze on her, she shivered. How many hours as a teenager had she fantasied about kissing him? How many ways had she thought to capture his interest, his attention?

"What kind of pie?" His voice was slow, lazy almost. The threads of anger barely kept beneath the surface.

She listed the four remaining choices. "Each pie was made fresh this morning. The cherry is especially good," she finished. She smiled again, curiously pleased she'd recognized him and he didn't have a clue who she was. Probably because he had not spent endless days and nights imagining all sorts of romantic scenes in which she featured prominently.

"I'll have a piece of the cherry, then," he said, tapping his fingers impatiently on the counter.

Once he'd been served, Lindsay didn't return to her table

in the back. Again her eyes sought the clock. Five minutes to closing, but he wouldn't be finished by then. She sighed softly and rubbed her back. The longer she was pregnant, the more her body ached at the end of each day. She'd be glad to have the baby, even though an entire new set of problems would present themselves.

"You should sit down," he said. "In fact, you probably should be home in bed. What are you doing working so late?"

"It's my job." Fussing with the condiments on the counter, she glanced at Luke from beneath her lashes. From the expensive clothes to the gold watch to the designer haircut, this man reeked money. She remembered his car when they'd been younger, too fancy for her family. What did he know of scarcity? Of making ends meet while trying to pay medical bills? Of the constant fear of what would happen to her and her baby if something unforeseen occurred?

He studied her as he ate, his eyes flicking impatiently from the cherry pie to her.

"Not married?" he asked, glancing at her left hand.

Surprised he would notice her bare finger, much less comment on it, Lindsay paused, then slowly shook her head, feeling mesmerized by his intense gaze. "No, I'm—"

"Lindsay, does the customer want anything from the grill? I'm about ready to shut it off," Jack called from the kitchen.

"No, he's just having pie. Go ahead," she returned.

She could tell Luke that she was a widow, that her husband had died almost eight months ago, but it wasn't any of his business. The wedding ring she cherished so much hung on a chain around her neck, had since her fingers had become too swollen to wear it comfortably.

In fact her entire body felt swollen and awkward. Her feet and ankles were three times their normal size. Retaining water, her physician had said, and recommended she stay off her feet as much as possible. Right, with her job?

She looked up and met his gaze. Heat blossomed through her as she held it, refusing to be the first to look away. Without being aware of it, a hint of challenge filled her gaze. She didn't like the idea he didn't remember her.

"Do I know you?" he asked, his eyes moving away from hers, searching each feature of her face.

"We haven't met in a long time," she said slowly. "Remember Manly Beach, about a dozen years ago?"

The frown on his face let her know he was still puzzled.

"Manly Beach?" he said ruminatively. "I haven't been there in years." He stared at her. his expression clearing. "You're little Lindsay McDonald."

Slowly she nodded, wondering if his memories would be similar to hers. She'd had a monstrous crush on him as a teen and had her heart broken when she reached fifteen.

"What the hell are you doing here?" he asked, his eyes flicking disparagingly over her uniform. His eyes pausing briefly on her extended waist.

Tilting her chin, she said coolly, "I work here, isn't that obvious?"

"But not married?" he said silkily.

She shrugged, ready to tell him about her husband. About the accident that had robbed her and her unborn baby of so much. But before she could speak he spoke again.

"Want to be?"

"I beg your pardon?" Had her mind wandered? What was he talking about?

"Do you want to be married when your baby comes?" he asked impatiently. Anger seemed to seep out of him. Tension almost shimmered in waves. He flung off his topcoat and crumpled it on the stool beside him. Yanking loose his tie, he took another gulp of the hot black coffee, his eyes narrowing as he stared at her.

"I don't think that's going to happen," she said slowly. Will was dead, had been gone for eight long and lonely months. He wasn't ever coming back. She would never see her husband again.

"It's important a child have a name," Luke stated.

"He'll have a fine name." Her temper flared. Did he think she couldn't provide for her child? Or that Will's name was somehow not good enough? He knew nothing about her! Of course—he thought she was still Lindsay McDonald. She needed to set him straight.

He turned and surveyed the table she'd been sitting at. Then looked at her. Was it possible his eyes were even darker?

"Are you in school?"

Nodding, Lindsay saw no reason to deny the obvious. "University."

"Are your folks helping out?" he questioned.

"You know, Luke, my private life is really none of your business. It's good to see you again after all this time, but I'm tired and want to go home. If you have finished your pie and coffee, I'll take payment and close for the night." Go home and think about Luke Winters, the boy she'd adored and the young man who had left never to return. And wish maybe in the deepest parts of her heart that she could have looked slim and glamorous when they met again.

"Must mean they're not."

"Only because they've been dead for almost ten years," she snapped, reaching for the empty pie plate. She scooted it through the pass-through to the kitchen. Jack could let it soak overnight. The rest of the kitchen crew had already left. When she reached for his cup, Luke's hand clamped down on her wrist.

"I'll have another cup of coffee," he said softly, daring her to deny him. "I'm sorry about your parents, Lindsay."

Lindsay swallowed, feeling a curious tingling pulse through her arm from the heat of his hand. Her entire body grew warmer. For a moment she forgot she was almost nine months pregnant, retaining water and so tired she could scarcely stand. For a moment she was aware of her femininity, of the tangle of feelings she'd always felt around Luke Winters—even after all the intervening years.

Nodding, she tugged and found herself instantly released. The pot wavered as she poured the coffee, reflecting the trembling that took over when he touched her.

Avoiding his eyes, she wiped the surface near his place and then leaned against the counter, raising her left foot and rotating it, trying to ease the discomfort. She was no longer a teenager with a crush. She had responsibilities, obligations. And if she had not attracted the man when they'd been kids, she sure couldn't do it now!

"You look tired," he said.

"If you'd finish, I could close and go home," she replied, flashing him another look. Their lives were vastly different. Had always been so, even as children, but the summers at the beach had minimized the difference. He played with the older boys. She and her friends had followed them, first pestering them for attention, then flirting. But she'd known, even then, that they were worlds apart.

Holding her gaze, he shrugged. "First, let me propose a deal."

"A deal?" Lindsay knew she was too tired to think straight, but she couldn't imagine any kind of deal she could make with Luke Winters. He probably bought and sold small countries in his spare time.

"How would you like to quit this job, continue your studies and not have to worry about money for the foreseeable future?"

"What do I have to do, sell my firstborn?" Instinctively, she covered the baby with her hands, as if guarding her precious child from the man before her.

"No. Just get married."

"Get married?" Her eyes widened. Had she heard him correctly? "And just who would I have to marry?" Instantly suspicions took hold. Was this some kind of black market deal? What did she really know about Luke? She hadn't seen him or spoken to him in over a decade. He'd been wild and determined as a teenager. What kind of man had he become? Stepping back, she put more distance between them. Suddenly glad to have Jack so close, she wondered if she could get rid of Luke without any trouble.

"You would have to marry me."

Stunned, Lindsay stared at him. "You are not serious," she said slowly.

"Very serious." For a moment the anger that simmered below the surface reemerged, but he clamped down on it. The flashing lights in his eyes warned Lindsay that he would be dangerous to cross. This was not the arrogant boy at the beach, but a man somewhere around thirty, who looked dark and dangerous. What had the past decade done to him?

"Have you been drinking?" she asked warily.

"A bit, but I'm not drunk, if that's what you think. Mad as hell, and out for revenge, but not drunk," he muttered. Nailing her with his gaze, he stared deep into her eyes. "Think about the deal I'm proposing. I'd give you an allowance, adequate to afford anything you want. You could quit work and stay home with your baby. Anything you'd need, I'd provide."

"And in exchange, what do I provide?" Somehow she couldn't see him interested in her as a wife, or in any way, for that matter. She was at the end of her eighth month of pregnancy, bloated with retained water, her blond hair lank and tied back in a serviceable ponytail. She knew she had circles beneath her eyes, she saw them every morning when she dragged herself from bed to get to her first job. The uniform she wore to work was misshapen and stretched beyond its original intent. Luke could not want her in his bed, but what did he want? Why propose marriage to someone like her? With his looks, money and family background, he could find a dozen women who would leap at the opportunity to become his wife.

"You provide me with a wife," he said grimly.

"I don't get it." She was too tired to think clearly.

"I want to get married—to pick my own wife. And I choose you."

"You don't know the first thing about me."

"Lindsay, we spent several summers at the same place. You followed me like a puppy for two summers. I know who your parents were and I know you are not married. That's all I need to know. I want a wife, you could use a husband. It would be strictly platonic. And I'd see you were taken care of financially, which will give you time to spend with your baby."

The silence stretched out between them. Lindsay tried to focus on the words, but they drifted around and around in her mind. She was so tired! Was she imagining his offer? She had to be. Why would he make such a ludicrous suggestion?

"Let me think about it," she said. Appalled at the words, nonetheless she didn't retract them. He had been drinking, maybe more than he admitted. It was obvious that the Friendly Corner Café wasn't the kind of eating establishment he was used to. Once he slept it off, he'd forget all about tonight. Appeasing him now would insure he'd leave soon, and without any trouble. She owed it to those long-ago summers.

Luke studied her expression and nodded. "I can see the notion never occurred to you. It obviously never occurred to my grandfather or mother, either. Damn it, I'll choose my own bride if it's the last thing I do! I'll be back tomorrow for your answer. Think about it until then. I will make no demands, and expect none in return. The only difference to the way things are now is that we would be married and you wouldn't have to work nights."

"That doesn't seem like much. Especially if you're going to be doing all the supporting. Babies aren't cheap." She couldn't believe she was acting as if his proposal was legitimate. Or that she was actually considering it. But for a moment the fantasy filled her. What a tantalizing dream it would be if she didn't have to worry about money, if she could stay home with her baby for the first few months and not be terrified of where they would live or what they would eat. She had so little money in reserve, so little strength, if it be known. It would be so easy to let someone else step in and help out for a little while. And it wasn't as if she didn't know Luke, or had known him once. But it was a long time ago, and people changed.

"Believe me, it's enough. Do you want references or something to make a decision?"

Lindsay smiled and shook her head. "No, I wouldn't need that." She would probably not see him again, but she'd play along for tonight.

"Think about it. I'll come tomorrow for your answer," Luke said, standing. He peeled off several large bills and dropped them carelessly on the counter. "Thanks for the coffee and pie, Lindsay."

Watching him leave the café, Lindsay felt various emotions churning inside, disbelief the strongest. He couldn't be serious. Had he had too much to drink? No one offered marriage to a stranger. They had nothing in common twelve years ago, had nothing in common now. Slowly she drew the cup and saucer from the counter and slid them into the kitchen. "I'm locking the front door now, Jack," she called, still dazed with what had transpired.

Quickly she went through the closing routine, gathered her books and headed for the kitchen to get her coat. The echo of Luke's bizarre proposal resounded in her head.

"I'll walk you part way," Jack said, pulling on a heavy coat. "And carry your books. You almost finished with the term?" The older man worried about her in his gruff way.

"My last exam is tomorrow. I won't be going next term." She would have her baby by then and needed every bit of money to make ends meet.

"You'll get your degree one day, Lindsay. You're a hard worker, I'll say that."

Smiling, she tucked her hand into his arm and the two of them started toward the bus stop.

"Who was the bloke who came in at the end?"

"Someone I knew as a child. Luke Winters," Lindsay said. "I haven't seen him in years." And somewhere along the way had stopped dreaming about the man. But she'd once thought she'd love him forever.

"He look you up?"

"No, actually, he didn't recognize me at first. But the strangest thing—" She hesitated, not knowing whether to give voice to the strange proposal Luke had made. He'd been drinking, probably blurted it out without thinking.

"What?" Jack asked, peering at her in the dark. The streetlights gleamed ahead. Soon the bus would arrive to take her home.

"He asked me to marry him."

"Good for him."

"Jack, you don't even know him."

"No, but I know you would be better off married to some bloke and staying home nights with that baby than trying to keep up at the café. Do you like the guy?"

"Yes, maybe. Actually, I haven't seen him in almost twelve years."

"So, maybe he was carrying the torch all these years."

Lindsay laughed gently. "I doubt it. It seemed like a spur-of-the-moment suggestion. I think it's a joke."

"Men don't ask women to marry them as a joke," Jack said gruffly.

"Rich men like Luke Winters don't ask waitresses to marry them, either."

"Like I said, maybe he's carried a torch for you all these years. How do you feel about him?"

Lindsay was silent for a long time, her mind racing with memories and emotions. How did she feel? "I had a crush on him when I was fourteen. But that was a long time ago. We went separate ways. I met Will."

"Listen up, girl. You and Will had a fine marriage, from

what you said, but it wasn't the grand passion that everyone yearns for.''

"You yearn for grand passion?" Lindsay said, startled.

"Not so much now, but everybody does at one point. You and Will hooked up, and had he lived, you would probably have been content all your life. But he died. And the marriage was more friends tying the knot than grand passion.''

"I loved Will," she protested.

"I know you did, but I never thought you were in love with the man."

Lindsay stared down the road, watching for the bus. His words were hard to take, but there was a grain of truth in them. She'd loved her husband. Now mourned his passing. But even at their happiest, she had sometimes wondered if there wasn't something more. Something missing from their relationship. Could Jack be right? Could she have loved Will as a friend but not been in love?

She had never felt the heights and depths with him she had as a teen with Luke. But she had attributed that to teenage hormones. Had something been missing?

Fog hovered in the sky, carrying the cold damp hint of salt from the harbor. Lindsay shivered slightly, glad to see the lights of the bus in the distance. Living on the main bus route insured she had a ride even late at night. But if she missed this bus, she'd have a long wait. The buses didn't run frequently this late.

"Your bus will be here in another minute. Think about this long and hard, Lindsay. You've had a few months alone. Just maybe this is a solution to your problems. You'd get to spend time with your baby and not have to worry about money. You like the man, don't you?" Jack asked.

She nodded. She'd been crazy about him as a kid. But she hadn't seen him in years. And it wasn't as if he proposed happy ever after. Just a marriage of convenience— mostly his convenience.

"I'll think about it, I guess," she said slowly. As if she had a choice. She would never forget the bizarre proposal.

Luke Winters strode along the street, ignoring the cold air that caressed his throat. The topcoat was small concession to the weather, especially worn like a cape. The heat from his anger warmed him. Damn his grandfather and his mother and their blasted machinations! The long walk from the opera house hadn't helped. The whiskey he'd consumed at that bar hadn't helped. Even meeting Lindsay McDonald at that café hadn't helped. Dammit, he was still furious. And he wasn't sure who made him the maddest, his mother, his grandfather or Jeannette.

He'd thought Jeannette wanted to marry him for himself, not his money. Or rather for his grandfather's money. Now he knew the truth, and it burned him up.

The old man had bribed her with promises of a portion of Balcomb Enterprises. Running his fingers through his hair, Luke stormed down the deserted sidewalk. He knew his grandfather wanted him married. The old man had pushed enough over the last ten years. And the latest maneuvers with the company about drove him crazy. But he'd gone too far with this trick.

His mother was positively obsessed by the subject of his marriage—but to the *right* woman. For them to go to such extremes was inexcusable. Luke would choose his own bride! And show them where their plotting led.

So he chose—a waitress from some café near the waterfront. Lindsay McDonald. He smiled grimly. Great. Maybe the whiskey had addled his brains. That or the anger.

He remembered his mother's dislike of his hanging out at Manly Beach as a teenager. At the popular beach, the rich and protected mingled with the rest of the Sydneysiders. He'd played up that aspect, rebellious as a teenager and pushing the limits his mother tried to impose. Seemed nothing had changed. Here he was tonight, still flouting his mother and her restrictions.

He could imagine her expression when he told her he would be marrying a waitress. Grimly he smiled. It would put paid to her scheming for entry into Sydney's highest echelons of society. If his grandfather's money hadn't bought her entrée into the level she wanted, his marriage certainly wouldn't. She'd be furious. For a moment the anger abated a bit. It would prove to be a small thing, but something that was sure to avenge her machinations.

He remembered Lindsay from those long-ago summer days. Her hair had almost bleached white in the sun, light freckles had dusted her cheeks, long coltish legs on a thin body had sported a deep tan. She'd been a pest most of the time. But there was something about her now that invited a second look, even as pregnant as she was. Maybe it was her air of defiance against all odds, or the fact she was going to school and holding down a job when she looked about to deliver at any moment. What happened to the baby's father? Skipped out, probably, once he knew a kid was on the way.

Luke's pace slowed as he drew near the opera house. The familiar billows gleamed in the foggy night sky, illuminated by spotlights. The street was practically deserted. Only a few couples lingered. The limo would have left long ago, taking his mother and Jeannette home.

Odd he didn't feel anything but anger. Shouldn't there have been a pang to discover the woman he'd asked to marry him had turned out to be in it purely for the money? But the anger that had poured through him at the discovery still blazed strong, overriding all the other feelings—except for satisfaction. He'd put paid to his family's scheming by marrying Lindsay McDonald. That would show the old man Luke Winters was not to be trifled with. His mother should have known all along. Hadn't he gone his own way for years now? Once his grandfather was convinced of Luke's determination to manage his own life, Luke could get a quiet annulment and be free.

He would not be dictated to by anyone! Somehow that

message had been missed by his grandfather and his mother. His marriage would show them the error of their ways.

Lindsay awoke the next morning to her alarm. Dragging herself from bed, she hastily dressed in her Tuesday dress. Money was too tight to afford a large selection of maternity clothes, so she had one for each day of the week. She was heartily sick of each outfit, but resigned to wearing them the remaining weeks of her pregnancy. Not much longer, thank God.

Brushing her hair, she wondered if it would ever regain its glossy shine. Dull and lifeless, at least it appeared neat and tidy tied back. She put on some makeup, trying vainly to hide the dark circles beneath her eyes. Her cheeks were plump, and her eyes looked red and tired and burned as she studied herself in the mirror. She almost laughed, her huge smile reflecting the humor of last night. As if Luke Winters, heir to a fortune, would seriously want to marry someone like her. Sleek and sophisticated, if he wanted to marry, he could find a willing woman almost anywhere in Sydney, and one certainly more attractive than she was at the moment.

Lindsay fixed oatmeal for breakfast and ate slowly, daydreaming about accepting his proposal. He'd give her lots of money, and she could afford a nice flat—one with a yard where she could take the baby in the summer. She'd have tons of new clothes and be able to buy a fancy crib for the baby, instead of searching the secondhand shops for a bargain.

No more working at the bookstore in the morning, attending classes in the afternoon and waiting tables at night. She'd become a lady of leisure, except for caring for her baby. Her eyes welled with tears. It was all fantasy.

She missed Will. He would have been so happy about their baby. She couldn't believe he was gone, that she'd never see him again. He'd been so nice! But the conversation with Jack played in her mind. They had loved each other, but had they really been in love?

They had been two lonely orphans drawn together by mutual interests. It was Will who had insisted she return to school to get a degree. His job had provided enough for the basics, and her part-time job at the bookstore had been enough to enable her to pursue an education. Everything had been fine until the truck with defective brakes crashed into Will's car. If the transportation company had kept the truck in good repair, the accident would never have happened.

But she couldn't change the past any more than she could predict the future. Rinsing out her bowl, Lindsay resolutely banished her daydreams. It was time to start for work. Firmly pushing away the tantalizing thought of Luke Winters, she concentrated on what she had to do today. After her morning shift at the bookstore, she had her last exam in the afternoon. She'd go home to change and be at the café early enough to eat a good dinner. After today things would ease up a bit. She could nap afternoons instead of attending class. That would help. And maybe some of the swelling would go down.

By the end of her shift at the café, Lindsay was glad she had not given any credence to Luke's wild offer the previous night, though she couldn't deny the niggling disappointment. The man had not shown up as promised. She kept telling herself she was not surprised, and definitely not disappointed, but a vague dissatisfaction lingered. For a moment, maybe just one moment, she had hoped the offer sincere. But she knew nothing in life came free, and his proposal had sounded too good to be believed. So much for fantasy and daydreams. The practical truth was she still had to work two jobs and save every penny she could manage. In another month she would be unable to work. She needed to build a nestegg.

The next night, at the height of the evening rush, Luke Winters entered the café as bold as brass. He paused in the doorway, surprised at the crowd. Feeling like a fool, he wondered why he thought a café would be empty at the dinner hour. It came from remembering the other evening, obviously, when it had just been the two of them. He scanned the room. Spotting Lindsay, he threaded his way through the tables until he stood beside her. She almost dropped the plates she carried as she stared at him in surprise. He looked at her, noticing how tired she looked, how awkward carrying the loaded plates.

"Can we talk?" he asked, glancing around the full café. There was a single empty table in the back corner near the swinging door that led to the kitchen. Frowning, he knew he'd timed things badly. But, impatient, he couldn't wait.

"I'm working right now." She stepped around him and headed for a table. Carefully placing the plates before the customers, she smiled and asked if they wanted anything else.

When they shook their heads, she turned and bumped into Luke. His hands reached out to steady her. She didn't quite reach his chin. Her hair was pulled back and tied at the nape of her neck. The sweet scent of roses wafted in the air. Her perfume? For a moment he was struck with how slight her build was—it was only her pregnancy which made her seem huge.

"Sorry, but you have a leading edge that's hard to miss," he said, looking at her stomach. He'd never been so close to a pregnant woman before. Was the baby heavy? Did it move around while she was working, or only when she was quiet?

"What do you want?" she asked, aware of the curious eyes of her customers. "I've got work to do."

"I want to talk about our wedding." He looked around. "Can you take a few minutes off?"

"Our wedding?" She stared at him in surprise.

Luke narrowed his eyes. "Yes, our wedding."

"I'm working, and it's not time for my break. Sit over

there and I'll get you something. I'll join you as soon as I can.'' She glanced around as if worried a customer was listening.

For the next thirty minutes Luke cooled his heels, watching the woman he intended to marry scurry around the café. He drummed his fingertips on the table, hiding the impatience that made him yearn to snatch her out of the café and take her somewhere quiet where she could focus solely on him and his proposition. She must know most of the customers, he thought, frowning. She had a word with each of them in passing, stopping from time to time to talk for several minutes. And she seemed well liked. Not that any of it mattered. He planned to marry her and leave her to her own devices.

His grandfather insisted on marriage before turning full control of his company to his only grandson. It had been his last-ditch effort to get Luke to conform to his idea of marriage stabilizing a man. Luke was incensed with the terms. He'd been working for months on a deal that would take Balcomb Enterprises to the forefront of the field, only to be blocked from the final stages by a stubborn old man who thought he could manipulate his only grandson. If they didn't act soon, the months of negotiation would be lost, and they would never be able to regain their advantage.

His grandfather had made no mention of any conditions beyond marriage. His mother was more focused in her intent. She wanted the perfect wife, with money and the right family. She saw Luke's marriage not only appeasing her father, but also gaining her additional cachet in Sydney. She wanted him to be aligned to one of the oldest and most prominent families in Australia.

Marriage gave a man stability, his grandfather insisted. Luke was thirty-two years old, had his own home in Kirribilli and a strong business background from the years spent with the firm. But if marriage was the price to gain control over the company he'd spent his entire adult life working for, then he'd pay it, and demand his grandfather comply with his conditions to grant Luke full control of Balcomb Enterprises.

As for his mother, he would be married. That fact alone would stop her machinations and probably fuel her anger. But it couldn't match his own. He made his own decisions. Time his family realized it once and for all.

Lindsay glanced at Luke and almost panicked. He hadn't forgotten that bizarre proposal. It hadn't been a drunken whim. He was serious about getting married. She tried to ignore the feelings that bubbled up, but the predominant one, relief, was too strong. How she wished she could let go and give in, to lean against his strength and let this man take care of her and her baby for a few months. If all he wanted was a paper marriage, why not? It would solve so many of her problems and give her the breathing space she needed. She felt raw and vulnerable with the immense responsibility of the baby looming. The fact was she faced an uncertain future all on her own, with no family to fall back on. She almost believed the proposal was a miracle. But there had to be a catch, she knew that.

After serving her customers, she stood as straight as she could, massaging her lower back, and walked over to him.

"Sorry you arrived when I couldn't talk," Lindsay said, slipping into the chair across from Luke. Tonight he wore a dark blue suit, light blue shirt and a silvery tie. He looked successful, commanding, arrogant—and as out of place in the café tonight as he had been in a tux two nights ago.

"I should have called first, but to tell you the truth, I've been searching for this place for two days. I just located it before I walked in."

"Searching for it?"

He nodded, his eyes brooding and watchful. Lindsay wished he'd smile just once. She hadn't seen a smile since he had been a young man. His face had altered slightly in the intervening years—the planes and angles sharper, more masculine. She could feast her gaze on him all night, yet the flutter in her heart concerned her. She could not be attracted to such a man. They had nothing in common but a few shared summers at the beach years ago.

And she was about to deliver a baby. Definitely not some man's fancy.

"Let's just say I forgot where it was, and it took me until now to find it again."

"Let's just say you were probably drunk on Monday night and stumbled into this place for coffee. No wonder you couldn't find it yesterday," she snapped, upset that she felt anything around this stranger. She was a fool if she continued talking with him.

"The fact is that I did find it, and you. Now I'm ready to talk marriage. You said you were going to think about it. Did you think I was joking when I didn't show up yesterday?"

"I thought you were joking on Monday night, truth to tell," she said slowly. She eased off her shoes and wiggled her toes. She was so tired of retaining water. Would she ever be back to normal?

"I never joke about marriage," he said grimly.

"Jack said men didn't."

"Who's Jack?" he asked sharply.

"The cook. Tell me you're still serious. Honestly, Luke, I don't understand any of this."

"I need a wife. For reasons I won't go into right now, I'm determined to choose my own wife. I choose you." He reached into his suit jacket and drew out a small packet of papers. He set them on the table and pushed them across to Lindsay.

"This is the proposed prenuptial agreement. Read it and see if there is anything you'd like changed. If not, we can get married tomorrow."

"Wait a minute! I never said I would marry you," Lindsay protested, dazed at the speed at which he moved. She was still trying to decide to take his remarks seriously, and he was talking about a wedding in the morning.

"You said you were thinking about it." His gaze narrowed. "Or was that just a way to placate me—to get rid of me without causing a scene?"

"I did think about it," she murmured, her eyes on the stack of papers, unwilling to confirm his suspicions. She'd thought of nothing else for two entire days. Slowly she reached out and drew the packet close. Unfolding, she began to read.

Stunned, she reread the first paragraph, quickly skimming the rest, then going back to carefully read word by unbelievable word. The man must be worth a fortune! He proposed to give her an allowance that was double what she and Will together had earned. She would receive the allowance for the duration of the marriage and for a year after it terminated.

She raised her eyes and stared at Luke. "I still don't understand. I get an allowance, a very generous one, I might add, just for marrying you?"

"That's right."

"For how long?"

"As long as I want."

"And the reason for this is what? I think I ought to know before making any commitment." Lindsay couldn't believe she said the words. First the other night, now tonight. Was she really tempted to accept his bizarre offer? And if so, was it truly for security for her baby, or to live out an almost forgotten fantasy?

Luke leaned back in his chair, the picture of a confident male. But the narrow gaze in his eyes led Lindsay to believe he cared more about what he planned to tell her than he wanted to reveal.

"My grandfather is Jonathan Balcomb. Maybe you've heard of him?"

"Balcomb Transportation!" She almost hissed the words. "One of their trucks caused my husband's death."

Luke sat up, thunderstruck. "What did you say?"

"My husband was killed almost eight months ago by a

Balcomb truck—one that was weeks overdue in maintenance and whose brakes failed," Lindsay said quietly.

"I thought you said you weren't married."

"You assumed that. And I guess technically I'm not. I'm a widow."

Luke didn't move, but Lindsay knew his mind was working furiously. Of all people to offer help for her baby, the grandson of the man whose company killed her baby's father! What irony. She tossed the papers in the center of the table and pushed back.

Luke rubbed his jaw thoughtfully, looked away, then at Lindsay. "Will Donovan?"

She nodded, surprised he knew Will's name. "I'm Lindsay Donovan. I was going to tell you the other night, but you were so sure you knew I was an unwed mother, I just—"

"Upon my marriage, my grandfather will turn the running of Balcomb Enterprises over to me completely. Balcomb Transportation is one of the companies under the corporate umbrella. I didn't realize it was your husband who had been killed last year."

"Do you work for Balcomb now?" she asked, carefully studying his face, her heart beating double time, her fingers trembling slightly. She should get up and walk away, but something held her in place.

"For the import-export branch for years but I am fully aware of the status of each division. Balcomb Enterprises is comprised of several companies, all working together."

"I don't like big business, I don't like cutting corners to make more profit, and I hate the idea of your grandfather's company getting away with a slap on the wrist in the way of a fine for killing my husband."

Luke studied her for a long moment. "Marry me to give me control of the company. When I get it, I'll make sure that every truck is serviced before its time and that we never let a defective vehicle leave the yard," Luke promised, his gaze firmly on her.

She stared at him. "Is this your way to throw a dog a bone?"

"No, it's my way to get control of my own life. My grandfather wants me to marry. He's throwing up roadblocks in the business until I comply. I've worked there for almost ten years and don't want to see the progress halted because of stupid manipulations.

"My mother also wants me to marry. I learned on Monday night that the woman I thought I had chosen for my wife, a woman I thought cared for me, was marrying me for my money and a hefty bribe my grandfather offered."

"No wonder you were so angry that night," she murmured.

"I'm proposing a business deal, Lindsay. Marry me. I'll take care of you and your baby and get control of the firm I've worked hard to build up over the last decade."

It almost made sense.

"With that control, I can insure senseless deaths like your husband's don't happen again. Do we have a deal?" Luke asked, leaning across the table, his eyes boring into hers.

She picked up the papers once more and reread them, the noise from the café fading as she read the terms. It was a deal made in heaven for her. She would have the security she lacked and the means to spend time with her precious baby when it was born. And somehow it seemed justified because the family that caused her husband's death would now be the family supporting her and her baby.

At least temporarily. Until Luke wanted his freedom.

She took a deep breath. "I guess we have a deal, Luke. I'll marry you whenever you say."

CHAPTER TWO

Four months later

LINDSAY laid Ellie down in the crib and patted her back. The baby was tired and fell asleep almost before Lindsay tiptoed from the nursery. Smiling, she shook her head. Some days Ellie couldn't be stopped with a tank. Today, her little girl had grown sleepy from their walk in the park, the fresh air and sunshine, and made no move to protest her nap. Lindsay just wished every day were so easy.

The doorbell rang, and she glanced over her shoulder. Nothing would wake Ellie before she'd had enough sleep. And even though she slept through the night, she seemed to need her naps as much as ever.

Lindsay crossed the sparsely furnished living room and went to the door. She opened it and stopped dead in surprise. The last person she'd expected to see was her husband!

"Luke," she whispered as she stared. Suddenly trepidation exploded. Why was he here? In the four months since their hasty wedding, she had not seen him. Immediately after the ceremony, he'd been called to handle a touchy labor problem with a subsidiary firm in England. He'd apologized profusely about the trip, swearing he'd return quickly. Only he hadn't.

His mother had stopped by the old apartment two days before Ellie's birth. Catherine Winters had made it clear she didn't approve of Luke's new wife. There had been no invitation to visit his home, no welcome to his family. Though from the little Luke had told her, she hadn't expected anyone to welcome her with open arms. She knew she was the spanner in the works to all their plans.

But she had expected to hear from Luke before this.

Promptly at the first of each month his check arrived, unaccompanied by a note or letter. She had called him when the baby was born, despite the time zone changes and difficulty in locating him. He'd sent a huge bouquet of flowers and a large teddy bear for the baby. When she found her new apartment, she'd dropped a polite note to his office address. Beyond that, there had been little communication between them except for brief calls now and then, which did nothing but offer an air of surrealism to their mock marriage. Now he stood as large as life in her doorway.

"This is an unexpected surprise," she said slowly. "Welcome back. Did you just get in?" Or had he returned to Sydney several weeks ago and was only now coming to see his hastily married wife?

"Lindsay?" he asked, disbelief evident in his tone and expression. His eyes raked her, from her tousled short curls to the slim body in the sundress down to her sandal-clad feet.

"Yes. Who did you think lived here?" she asked with some asperity. It was the shock. And the fear. Had he finally come to his senses and wanted out of the marriage? She knew it had been too good to be true, too good to last. No one got anything in life for nothing. Probably being away from his family for so many weeks brought him to his senses.

He stepped forward. Rather than be mowed over by him, Lindsay moved aside, gripping the doorknob like a lifeline. He was more imposing than she remembered. His black eyes swept the neat living room, and he moved toward the sofa as if assured of a welcome. He noticed the photos on the walls and on the table. Most were of Ellie, from a sleeping infant in the hospital crib to her in her pram. Lindsay's gaze flicked to her beloved photo of Will. Would Luke mind she had her first husband's photo on display? She wanted Ellie to have that, at least, since the baby would never know her father.

Slowly Lindsay shut the door. Luke had no reason to mind anything. She had lived up to her end of the agreement by marrying him. He had his paper wife. The terms had been his. He hadn't suggested she move into his house, nor had he suggested any kind of relationship between them.

"Have a seat. Would you like some tea?" she asked.

"If it's not too much trouble."

"No." She'd welcome the breathing space to get some sort of control over nerve endings that seemed jangled. What was he doing here? "I'll be right back."

"Fine." He sat on the sofa, already loosening his tie as she went into the kitchen, his eyes still on her.

Preparing the tea took a bit of time, minutes Lindsay used to take a few deep breaths and try to school her features into the impassivity Luke Winters seemed to manage so well. If their marriage was to end, so be it. She knew she lived in a fairy tale. No one paid a woman just to be married. She'd done nothing but stand before a judge and exchange vows. Meaningless ones. What had the terms of their agreement been? Where were the papers? When he left, she would reread them to see where she stood.

At least she'd managed to save quite a bit each month from the generous allowance he provided. It would be a start to see them through until she found a job. She'd loved these few months with her daughter, spending time with her, watching her grow. Though she hated the thought of giving her into someone else's care during the day, Lindsay scrambled around for an idea that would allow her to spend time with Ellie and still earn a living. Nothing came immediately to mind.

Taking the pot, the cups and saucers, she loaded the tray and headed into the living room. She had to face him, face the future. Hiding in the kitchen accomplished nothing.

"It's been a while since I carried a tray," she said brightly as she walked into the room. She would get through this. Maybe the café would hire her back. Jack said the new waitress wasn't as reliable as Lindsay had been.

Luke sat sprawled on the sofa, his long legs stretched out before him, crossed at the ankle, his fingers in the slash pockets at the side of his trousers, his suit jacket across the arm of the sofa. His tie had been loosened and hung crookedly across his broad chest. Luke Winters was sound asleep.

Lindsay stared at him as she carefully set the tray on the low table before the sofa.

"Luke?" she said softly.

There was no response.

She wanted to giggle, catching her lower lip between her teeth. She thought he'd come to let her know he wanted an annulment, to give notice her cushy life was about to end. Instead, it looked as if he just wanted a place to sleep.

Sitting quietly in the comfortable chair by the sofa, she studied the man. He looked older than she remembered, more than just the sixteen weeks since she'd seen him. There were new lines around his eyes, along his mouth. But his dark hair appeared as rich and thick as ever. His body seemed trim, if a bit thinner than she remembered, but maybe her memory was faulty. It had been a most peculiar time, and she had been so tired from work and her pregnancy she had trouble remembering a lot about those few days.

Whatever he had to say could obviously wait. Slowly she poured herself a cup of tea, sat back and sipped it, content to watch him until he awoke. Images danced in her mind—the first time she'd met him at the beach. How arrogant and overbearing he'd seemed—stuck up, she'd thought. She smiled, remembering how she'd break through that arrogance with her own infuriating taunts until he'd chase her along the water's edge. It had been a long time ago. She didn't have any images of recent events. Every-

thing about their wedding blurred. His mother and grandfather had not attended. Jack had been her only guest. He'd
looked Luke over and nodded, as if satisfied. Smiling in
memory of his vetting Luke, she still found the entire situation peculiar. Nevertheless, she was grateful to have the
chance to stay home with Ellie for these first months. She
wished she could do something in return for Luke, to thank
him for providing so well for her.

Luke grew gradually conscious, but didn't move. Refusing
to open his eyes was one way to avoid dealing with the
myriad of problems that faced him. He was so tired. Tired
and worried. What had once been viewed as challenging
now seemed tedious. People at work, at home, all demanded his time and attention—and wanted him to perform
miracles he could not do.

Yet he felt surrounded by peaceful quiet. He could hear
the faint ticking of a nearby clock. He had no clocks that
ticked. Slowly he lifted his lids, gazing from the narrow
slit at the woman sitting in a chair, leafing through a magazine.

Lindsay McDonald Donovan Winters, his wife.

She didn't know he'd awoken. How had he fallen asleep?
Granted, he'd been home from England only a few hours,
up most of last night, and then had met with the board of
directors at a hastily called board meeting early this morning. But he'd done things like that before and never fallen
asleep in someone's living room.

As he stared at the woman, he wondered if he were seeing things. She didn't look at all like the woman he'd married so hastily. As he remembered his wife, she was plump
with rather long, drab hair. This woman looked nothing like
her. Her frothy blond curls seemed almost to radiate a light
of their own, bright and silky-looking. He wanted to touch
them, see if those curls felt as soft as they looked.

His gaze moved down the delicate features of her face.
He was struck by the high cheekbones, the slight tilt to her

eyes. Her skin was as smooth as ivory and looked as soft as her hair. He could clearly see the young girl she'd been, chasing after him, teasing him, then laughing in joyful abandon. Continuing his perusal, he noted her high, firm breasts, the slender waist and soft swelling of her hips. She had tucked her feet beneath her on the chair, but he vaguely remembered thinking how sexy her legs were when she'd gone to prepare the tea.

Shifting his gaze, he noted the teapot and one used cup.

"Guess I slept through tea," he said slowly.

Her head came up and she looked at him, amusement lurking in her gray eyes. "I guess you did. Tired?"

He rubbed his face and sat up, looking at the teapot. "A bit. Is the tea still hot?"

"Probably not. You slept for over a half hour." She stood and reached for the pot. "If you can stay awake long enough, I'll fix another."

"I'll come with you." He rose and Lindsay turned. He watched as she walked into the kitchen. He'd been right about her legs. Following more slowly, he looked around her house. It had very little furniture. The only decorations appeared to be pictures of her daughter and an occasional knickknack on a table or shelf. There were stacks of books in one corner, and on the other wall a shallow bookcase. The television was small. He saw no signs of a stereo set.

Following her into the kitchen, he noticed it appeared as spotless as the living room. When he stepped closer, she moved away. Was she afraid of him? He frowned again.

"Do you take anything in your tea? Milk?" Lindsay asked.

"No, I like it black. How have you been?"

"Fine."

"Lindsay, I'm not just making small talk. I want to know how you have managed up to now. I didn't plan to stay away for so long. I thought I'd be back in just a couple of weeks. I was surprised to find you were living here. My mother was to come see you, offer you any help you needed while I was gone."

She faced him, tilting her chin slightly as if facing a problem. He almost smiled. Suddenly he was curious about this woman he'd made his wife and then ignored since their wedding.

"Thank you for what you've done, Luke. I truly appreciate it. We're managing very well on your generous allowance. And your mother did visit, but I don't think she was so pleased to find out I was the one you married. She remembered me as an urchin at the beach. Besides, we agreed that it would be a paper marriage only. I never expected help from your family. I imagine they aren't so pleased with your marriage."

"Sometimes tact isn't her strong point. I apologize if the interview was awkward," he murmured. For a moment he regretted sending his mother. He'd done it to drive the point home that he was married. But she'd been furious when she'd learned what he'd done. And he should have expected her to take that out on Lindsay.

He looked around at the sparseness of the furnishings. There were no appliances on the counter save the toaster. There were no rows of canisters, no gadgets.

"Is the allowance enough?"

"Plenty."

"You don't seem to have much furniture," he said slowly. He wasn't sure what was missing, but the flat looked half empty.

She laughed and shrugged. "We have enough. There are only two of us, and one is very small."

"Your baby."

"Ellie."

He nodded. He'd wanted to go see her in the hospital when he'd received the call, but he couldn't leave the UK at the time. He should have asked about the baby first thing. Didn't first-time mothers dote on their children?

"I'm a little late, but congratulations."

Lindsay beamed at him. "You said that on the phone. I loved the flowers. And she has your teddy bear propped up in the corner of her crib. You can see her later, if you like. She's sleeping right now."

He rubbed the back of his neck, stiff from his nap on the sofa. "Like father, like daughter, huh?" he said trying to lighten the atmosphere.

Lindsay's smile faded, and she stared at him.

"Sorry, just a joke. We were both napping."

"You're not her father," she said.

"Of course not, it was a bad joke, Lindsay. But you have to expect most people will think I'm her father, or stepfather at the very least."

She nodded, turning to take the kettle off the stove. She rinsed the teapot, filled it with hot water and turned to carry it into the living room.

"You should have waked me up," he said as she approached him.

"I figured anyone so tired they'd fall asleep that quickly in a strange place must need the rest. If you'd still been asleep at suppertime, I would have wakened you."

When they each had a cup of tea before them, Lindsay looked at him.

"Since this is the first time you've made any contact with me since the wedding, I assume you have something to say. Are you ready for the annulment?"

He glanced up, startled. Slowly he sipped the hot brew, holding her eyes over the rim of the cup. He placed it on the table and shook his head.

"No. I've come to ask a favor of you. And I'm willing to make it well worth your while."

"A favor, yet you plan to make it worth my while? What kind of favor?" She studied him with grave gray eyes.

"My grandfather is a very sick man. The doctors say he's dying," Luke said slowly. Even now he could scarcely believe it. The man had seemed in fine health before he'd left for England. And he'd always thought the old man too ornery to die.

"I'm sorry," she said.

He lifted an eyebrow. "They don't give him long to live, Lindsay. I had him moved to my home. I have a lot more room than he or Mother. We have a round-the-clock nurse, but at least he doesn't have to stay in hospital. There's nothing I can do for him. Except—"

"Except?" she prompted when he was silent for a long moment.

"Lindsay, when we got married, you knew it was to spite my mother and grandfather. To do what they insisted, but on my own terms."

She nodded. "I often wondered how things turned out when you told them you had married me. I know your mother was coldly furious. She made it clear that I was nothing but a gold digger and she'd do all she could to end this farce of a marriage."

He closed his eyes for a moment. "Sorry about that. I hadn't expected to leave so suddenly for London. Actually, you got off lightly. It was quite a scene when I told them. I went directly to my grandfather's home in Palm Beach after our ceremony. Not only was he there, so were my former fiancée, Jeannette, and my mother. I told them all at the same time. Jeannette swore I had ruined her life, ruined both our lives, ranting and raving as if I were the great love of her life, instead of a bank account. My grandfather swore he would never turn the company over to me. My mother was horrified, more by the loss of social status than anything, I think." He paused, remembering. In retrospect it almost seemed like some kind of bad comedy.

"And you?" she asked.

"I just swore."

She winced. "Not a good situation. You married to gain full control of the company. I'm surprised you didn't ask for the annulment before now, since you didn't get it."

"I'm not here about an annulment," he said sharply.

"You're not?"

"I got the company. When my grandfather threatened to cut me out, I called his bluff. I'm an excellent manager, Lindsay. I knew there were other companies out there that would pay top dollar to have me work for them. My grandfather taught me well, you see. So I said I didn't need his company, I would find another job."

"Wow, you were burning bridges left and right."

Luke's face hardened. "I won't be dictated to!"

"I'll remember that if I ever wish to issue an edict," she murmured, sipping her tea. The fatigue that cloaked him when he arrived had fled. He looked energized, confident, a bit arrogant. And still the best-looking male she'd ever seen.

"A month after our wedding, probably because of the negotiations I was doing in London, Jonathan relented. I was named chief executive of the conglomerate. I got the notice in London via fax."

"Congratulations."

He hesitated, looking at her suspiciously.

"What?"

Taking a deep breath, Luke continued. "Nothing. Along with the new position came a bit of a reconciliation with my grandfather. It wasn't until I learned of his illness and made plans to return home this week that I realized his health had caused the change, not my marriage or any attempt to make up. He had his first attack three months ago and knew he couldn't manage the firm any longer. Sometimes it takes a hard lesson for someone to learn something. I should mention he hasn't tried to interfere in any aspect of my life since the wedding. When he turned over control, he did it totally. But he mentioned he was not happy with our situation."

"Family is so important, Luke. I know, because I don't have one. Except for Ellie, of course. I'm sorry he's so ill. Is that why you returned home?"

"No, the business was settled in London. I came home

as planned, only discovering the full extent of his illness then. He refused to permit anyone to tell me while I was away. I had my secretary arrange for him to move from the hospital to my house, hire nurses, get specialists' opinions.'' He rubbed his eyes with his thumb and forefinger.

''He's lucky he has you,'' she said.

Luke looked up at her words. ''Why don't you have family? What happened to your parents, Lindsay?''

''They died in a plane crash shortly after our last summer at the beach. My mother's only sister raised me until I turned eighteen. Then she moved to Tasmania. A few years after that she died. She'd been ill for a while, and that prompted her move. She had always wanted to live in Tasmania and knew she had to get there before it was too late.''

''And your husband's family?''

''He was orphaned as a baby. No kin. Cherish your grandfather, Luke, you are lucky to have had him so long.''

''I want to make his final days happy, Lindsay.''

''I can understand that.''

''Even if he is the man responsible for your husband's death?''

She took a deep breath. ''He wasn't directly responsible. It was his company. Morally I feel he had some responsibility, but the manager who let the defective truck on the road is the real culprit.''

''I found out who it was and fired him, my first official act as head of the firm,'' Luke said quietly.

Her eyes widened. ''You did? Oh, Luke, thank you!''

''I still need a favor, Lindsay.''

''Name it,'' she said, wondering what he could ask of her. She had so little to offer.

''I want you to come home with me. Live with me as my wife and pretend we have a wonderful marriage that is filled with happiness—to ease the last days of a dying man.''

He almost laughed at her expression. Stunned disbelief

would be one description. Astonishment might be another. Total amazement came close.

"Live with you?" Her voice was high, unsteady. This was not part of their original agreement. Her heart rate sped up. Live with Luke? See him every day? Share meals with him, share their lives for a while? For a second she remembered the long-ago dreams of Luke as her knight in shining armor. This was not exactly how she expected those dreams to come true.

"You and the baby. My home is big enough. I've installed Jonathan in one of the bedrooms. There's a nurse on duty at all times. You wouldn't have any responsibilities in that direction. Just be available. Maybe talk to him once in a while, tell him how much you love me. You know, that kind of thing. Whatever the normal reasons are for a marriage. I want him to believe we're happy. It won't be for long."

"Are you crazy? Our agreement was total uninvolvement with each other. Your terms. Now you want me to pretend to be your wife, your loving wife? They'll never believe it."

"You are my wife. I just want you to act the part. Besides, I mentioned we had a thing going as teenagers, so I think they'll think we just rekindled our affair."

"I can't believe this."

Luke normally held out longer in negotiations, but this was too important. "We have an agreement that when our marriage ends, you walk away with nothing. I'm willing to change that. Set up a trust for you and your daughter. You'll be free to marry again if you choose, or not. But money won't ever be a problem again. Just come home with me and play a role until my grandfather dies."

"Do you think money can buy everything?" she asked, narrowing her eyes as she frowned at him. For a moment Luke wondered if she'd jump up and stamp her foot. He was taken aback at her vehemence.

"Money can buy most things. It bought me a marriage, didn't it?" he said sardonically.

She sat back abruptly at that. For a moment he thought he saw tears swimming in her eyes. But she never took her gaze from his.

"I want an annulment," she said firmly.

"Not yet. First you help me out." He'd thought she'd leap at the chance to get more money. What was wrong with her?

"No. I'm not tricking people."

"We did already." Scruples.

"No, we got married. That's all you wanted. You said that's all there would be."

"Things have changed."

"I haven't."

"Honey, you've changed the most. You don't look anything like the dumpy woman I married."

"Dumpy? I was pregnant!"

"And working two jobs and trying to go to school. Tell me, Lindsay, would you rather I hadn't followed through on my irrational proposal and married you? Would you rather have kept working two jobs and tried to raise your baby? What if you got sick, or she did?"

Lindsay swallowed hard. Her lips tightened into a firm line. Luke hoped she was trying to imagine the life she would be living had it not been for him.

"All I'm asking is your help to make my grandfather happy for the few weeks he has left. It shouldn't be too long." Luke swallowed. He didn't want to think about how frail Jonathan looked, how short a time remained. He should have been told months ago about Jonathan's illness. "And in exchange, I'll make sure you continue to spend the days with your daughter rather than waiting tables at some café."

"That makes me feel so mercenary," she muttered.

"No, mercenary is someone like Jeannette Sullivan. By now she would have demanded to know the amount of money I was offering and made counteroffers to raise the stakes. You never questioned the money. Even when we were married."

"It was more than enough for me," she said quietly.

"Where do you spend the money, Lindsay?" he asked, glancing around. "Not on furniture or things for the house."

"We have all we need," she said, fidgeting with the arm of the chair.

"So you said."

"I saved part," she said slowly, wondering if he'd want it back since she hadn't used it. No, he was too generous for that. He was offering her more to spend a little time at his home and pretend to his grandfather that they were happy together.

"How frugal."

"It was for...if you wanted...in case...for when we got the annulment."

"The day after we bury my grandfather, I'll start proceedings for the annulment if you want. Give me these few weeks, please."

"I need to think this over. You're pushing me to do something I'm not sure I can. We know nothing about each other, Luke. You want me to pretend an emotion that I don't feel? What about the rest of your family?"

"My mother is staying with me temporarily while her father is so ill. She knows I'm trying to talk you into coming home with me."

"I bet that went over well. She didn't like me as a kid. She's horrified you married me. Now you want me to come live in your home?"

"It's my home, and as you are my wife, it's your home, as well. You will run things there, not my mother. If having her stay there makes you uncomfortable, she can return to her home and come each day to visit her father."

"No, that's not what I mean. Does she know why we got married?"

"Yes. You're right, she won't welcome you with open arms. Jeannette was her choice. But she'll be cordial. My mother is always the proper lady. I'm not concerned about how she reacts. I want to give my grandfather some assurance that I have not made a mess of my personal life."

"Getting an annulment and marrying the woman of your dreams would make him very happy," she suggested.

"You are the woman of my dreams," he said, smiling broadly.

"Me?"

"Sure, what man wouldn't want a wife who keeps the other woman away by virtue of being a wife, yet is never around to curtail his own activities, never nags, never demands anything. You're an ideal wife."

She looked away as if trying to keep from smiling. "That would end if I moved in with you."

"I doubt that. You don't seem the demanding type. Lindsay, I want you to say yes."

She gazed at the pictures on the wall, and Luke wished he knew what she was thinking. She was right. They didn't know each other very well. If they did, maybe he'd have a clue to her thought process. He was already struck by the fact she still had not asked about the money, that she worried more about deceiving people than what she would get out of the deal. Most of the people he knew could care less about scruples. Hell, he himself didn't care, as long as it made Jonathan happy.

Slowly she turned back. "What would you tell your grandfather? We've been married for more than four months and never been together. Why the sudden change?"

She was going to do it! He knew it in his bones. Relief washed through him. Leaning back against the high sofa cushions, he relaxed a bit. The hard part was over. He'd convinced her to help him out!

"I've been out of the country for the entire time. Is it so hard to believe I would wait to move you into our home until I could live there with you? He doesn't need to know we haven't been in touch with each other since the wedding. He and I don't ordinarily live in the same house. I've kept him apprised from time to time about things you are doing. We'll just say that now that I'm back, you're moving in with me.''

"And you think he'll buy that?" she asked skeptically.

"Why not, if he sees us acting like we are in love."

She licked her lips. "And how is that?" she asked warily.

"You look at me as if you adore me. I'll come home for dinner every night. When we're in visiting with my grandfather, we'll hold hands or something. I don't know. Whatever seems right at the time."

"And the rest of the world? Your mother?"

"What?"

"What do we tell the rest of the world?"

"The same thing. I don't want anyone carrying tales to him that this isn't a real marriage, or that I'm not really happy. If you act your part well, he'll believe my tale of teenage feelings lasting. He's dying, Lindsay. He wants to see me happy. Can you be packed by late this afternoon? I'd like you to be there for dinner tonight."

"Today? Good grief, Luke, I haven't even said I'll do it."

"But you will, won't you, Lindsay? For Jonathan? And for your daughter?"

Several minutes slowly passed. Lindsay's eyes locked on Luke's as she considered his proposal. Finally she nodded. "I still feel like a cheap mercenary, but I'll do it. For your grandfather and my daughter. And for myself. I've felt guilty taking your money and doing nothing in return. Maybe this will balance things a bit."

"Good!" He jumped up and slung on his suit jacket. "I'll send a car around at four."

"I can't manage—" Lindsay rose and stood near him.

"Pack a few things for the next couple of days. On

Saturday, you and I'll come back and get everything you need."

"I think you are going too fast for me. I need time to think—"

"You can think at my house. The car will be here at four. I'll see you at dinner." Luke leaned over and brushed his lips across hers. "Thank you, Lindsay, I'll never forget this."

Lindsay watched in silence as he crossed the room and let himself out of the flat. Slowly she raised her fingers and rubbed them across her lips. She would never forget any of this, either. But probably for different reasons. Unbelievable—she had just agreed to live with the stranger who had been her husband legally for four months. And not just live with him, but pretend to be a devoted wife.

"Oh, Will, you wouldn't believe the mess I've gotten myself into!" But Will had been dead over a year now, and she had passed the worst of her grief. Only gentle memories of happier times remained.

Thankful Ellie still slept, Lindsay hurried into her room and began sorting through her closet, trying to decide what clothes she'd need over the next few days. She finished packing her things by the time the baby awoke. While Ellie cooed to herself and watched her mobile, Lindsay packed her clothes, including the teddy bear Luke had sent. She'd piled everything by the baby's pram at the door when the knock came.

A uniformed driver stood on the stoop when she opened the door.

"Mrs. Winters?" he asked formally.

Lindsay nodded, swallowing hard. She had not used Luke's name when they married, opting to keep Donovan, since she didn't really feel married. The driver was the first person to call her Mrs. Winters.

"There's rather a lot," she said, indicating the stack by the door.

"Not a problem, madam. It may take me a few trips.

When I get the last stowed, I'll return for you and the baby.''

A bit over a half hour later Lindsay arrived at Luke Winter's home in Kirribilli, located on the northern shore of the harbor, just a short drive from Harbor Bridge. The estate seemed huge to Lindsay, at least an acre in size. The long driveway swept before the house, ending in a half-circle. The imposing facade was patterned after Tudor England, with brick and stucco and dark exposed beams.

The driver escorted her to the front door. "I'll bring your things in," he said, ringing the bell firmly.

"Thank you." Lindsay felt almost tongue-tied. The baby stared at the man with huge eyes, sucking her thumb as she watched his every move. Her fascinated gaze seemed to absorb everything.

"Mrs. Winters?" A dark-skinned woman opened the door. She was petite, thin and by the predominance of gray in her hair not young. Her eyes were bright with curiosity.

"Yes."

"Welcome. Luke told us you'd be arriving today. I'm Marabel, the housekeeper. I can show you to your room, and the baby's. Once Hedley brings in your bags, I'll unpack."

"I don't mind unpacking for myself and the baby," Lindsay said quickly, scanning what she could see of the house. The wide stairs leading to the second floor were polished until they reflected the light spilling in from the tall windows. The open arch that led to the living room beckoned. She took a few steps into the room and knew why Luke had wondered about her sparse room. This one was filled to overflowing with furniture, paintings, carvings and figurines. Either he was a collector or someone had decorated the room for him.

"This way." Marabel led the way up the stairs, turning to the right at the top.

"Mr. Jonathan is in the far room down that hall."
She indicated the opposite end of the hall. "This is your
room. Yours and Luke's," she said, standing beside the
open door.

CHAPTER THREE

"WHERE's Ellie's room?" Lindsay asked, peeking into the huge master bedroom. All she seemed to see was the large bed that dominated one wall. Swallowing hard, she turned to Marabel. She had to talk to Luke and get this straightened out. Sharing a room had not been part of the deal!

"It's just beyond your room." Marabel moved down the long hall, opened a door and stood aside.

Lindsay stared at the elegant child's room. The crib looked brand new, made up with gaily decorated sheets. There was a soft mobile dangling above one end. A toy box stood near the window, and shelves lined one wall, filled with stuffed animals, dolls and children's books. A child's table and two small chairs sat in the corner, a rocking chair nearby. The room was filled with light from the tall windows outlined by pristine white curtains. The soft silver carpet on the floor would insure warm feet for a toddler or child. Had Luke thought they would stay that long?

"It's lovely." Lindsay held Ellie closely and studied the room.

"Luke ordered all the furniture and toys himself," Marabel said with some pride.

"When?" Lindsay asked. Slowly she crossed to the crib, leaned over and released the baby. Ellie's eyes seemed to roam around the room. Her gaze fastened on the mobile.

"It's been ready for the baby since yesterday. First place Luke went after arriving home was the baby store. He could have had it done by the staff, but I guess Luke wanted to do it himself. We figured you didn't want to move here until he was home," Marabel said.

Lindsay looked at her sharply. Touched at the trouble he'd gone to for someone who might not have come at all, she nodded. Had he been so sure of her answer?

"I'll see to Hedley. He'll bring your bags up," Marabel said.

Lindsay moved around the nursery once the housekeeper left, touching everything, watching Ellie.

"The difference between tons of money and scraping by," she murmured, lightly setting the mobile in motion. The furnishings she'd purchased for Ellie were secondhand, clean and serviceable, but they showed the scars of use. It had been all she could afford. She had never been comfortable with the arrangement she and Luke had made so hastily that evening. Fearing any day he would come to his senses and end their marriage, she had been frugal and cost conscious. Obviously Luke did not suffer the same consciousness.

Sitting in the rocker, she moved back and forth. Her daughter was too young to remember this when she grew up. But it was good to know that she'd enjoy the best money could buy for a while. And Lindsay would remember. She might be able to afford a bit more for Ellie if Luke set up a trust account for them.

He must love his grandfather a great deal. Was that why she agreed to this scheme? She felt little compassion for the old man. He had the reputation around Sydney of being a tough old bastard. And his way of squeezing a profit from any source, even neglecting the care and maintenance of his equipment, did nothing to redeem him in Lindsay's eyes. The responsibility for her husband's death in the end rested in Jonathan Balcomb's hands. It had been his company, after all.

So this charade wasn't to comfort an old man. And it wasn't the money, though it would help make life much easier. But she was young and could work like millions of other women. No, it had something to do with Luke and the way he wanted so much to do something for his grandfather. Despite the fact the old man had tried to manipulate him into a loveless marriage, Luke had forgiven him, drawn close in the face of adversity and now wanted to ease his grandfather's final days.

It was for Luke, Lindsay decided, and wondered if that made it any better.

"Come on, baby girl, let's explore this fantasy bedroom. Enjoy it while you can, it won't last forever." Lindsay pushed up from the rocker and went to pick up her daughter. Gazing out the window at the beautiful garden, she wondered how long they would stay. Would the flowers still be blooming when Jonathan's days ended? Or would winter arrive before then?

By the time Lindsay was ready to go down for dinner she was a nervous wreck. She'd found her way to the kitchen earlier, to get a spot of tea before feeding Ellie. Marabel had wanted the cook, Rachel, to stop dinner preparation to fix the tea, but Lindsay insisted she could manage. She was used to doing things for herself. She met Rachel, exclaimed in delight at the fresh scones and cream and promised her she'd bring down the baby as soon as she was awake. At least the staff was cordial.

Lindsay unpacked Ellie's clothes and folded them in the spacious chest of drawers. There were fresh diapers in one drawer, another sign of Luke's thoughtfulness. As she rocked the baby while Ellie nursed, Lindsay felt a moment of overwhelming panic. She should not be doing this. She couldn't continue to accept things from Luke and give so little back. They had to discuss that before the charade went too far.

Once Ellie finished, Lindsay gave her a bath and dressed her for bed. Rocking her to sleep was a pleasure both mother and child enjoyed. As Ellie's eyes drooped, Lindsay hugged her baby close. She was the only familiar thing in a house too big, too rich, too formal for Lindsay's tastes.

When Ellie slept, Lindsay placed her in the crib and covered her. She left the room quietly, wondering if Ellie would sleep through the night in a strange place.

"Of course, children are more adaptable," Lindsay murmured as she crossed the hall to the bedroom Marabel had pointed out earlier. Lindsay paused. She could smell the after-shave lotion Luke used. It instantly conjured up images of the man. Studying the masculine room, she knew it suited him perfectly. The bed was massive, but he was a tall man. Still, she thought as she stepped into the room, it would comfortably hold two or more people. For a moment she wished she were truly married, that the bed was one she and her husband shared. Mornings, when she was older, Ellie could run in and jump in bed with them, waking them up. They'd laugh and hug and be so happy.

She swallowed and turned from the vision. The dark drapery surrounding the windows on the wall didn't admit as much light as the curtains in Ellie's room. She wished she could open them wider, let the sun shine in, dispel some of the darkness. Richly polished furniture, deep carpets, a small sofa finished the decor. The paintings on the wall were strong and vibrant, two abstracts and two sea scenes. Luke's taste appeared eclectic.

Frowning, Lindsay looked for her bags. She knew Marabel directed Hedley to deposit them in this room. Had Luke moved them? Was he home yet?

Curious, Lindsay opened a closet door and saw a row of suits, dress shirts and jeans. Jeans? For leisure, she supposed. At the far end hung several dresses—her dresses.

So much for Marabel listening to the new mistress of the house. Lindsay had specifically said she'd unpack. Now she'd have to move all her clothes to whichever room Luke designated for her. Glancing at her watch, Lindsay decided the move could wait. Marabel had told her dinner would be ready at seven. It was already after six-thirty.

Lindsay pulled her best dress from the hanger and turned to the dresser. After opening and closing several drawers, she finally found her underwear. Grabbing what she needed, she hurried to the bathroom. A quick shower, don the dress she'd chosen, and she'd be as ready as she was going to get tonight. Obviously she and Luke needed to discuss more than a few things.

It was precisely seven o'clock when she descended the stairs. Lindsay saw the china and silver gleaming on the dining room table as she reached the foyer, but it was the murmur of voices in the living room that drew her attention. Pausing in the archway to the room, Lindsay swallowed hard, butterflies suddenly making their presence felt in her stomach. Luke stood before the fireplace, sipping an aperitif. Seated on the sofa was his mother. She was elegantly clad. Her dark hair was lightly sprinkled with gray, but stylishly cut and flattering. Her makeup was discreet, the dress a designer original. Gems glittered at her throat and fingers. Lindsay touched Luke's wedding ring, hung by a gold chain beneath the high collar of her dress, and took a deep breath.

"I hope I'm not late," she said, raising her head and stepping into the room.

The woman on the sofa turned and looked at Lindsay, eying her from top to toes. It was evident she found Lindsay lacking.

"You are not late. How are you?" Luke crossed the room and took her hand, squeezing it slightly as he leaned over and brushed his lips across her cheek.

Stunned at the tingling sense of awareness that ignited at his touch, Lindsay gripped his hand as she stared at him with surprise. "Fine." Did he feel this odd magnetic pull, as if her body were tuned to an electrical wave pattern he alone generated. If he felt the same sensation, he gave no sign. Lindsay looked away.

"Mother, I'd like you to welcome Lindsay home. Lindsay, you remember my mother, Catherine Winters." Luke drew her over to the sofa.

"So the forgotten bride finally makes an appearance."

Catherine Winters made no move to rise or greet her new daughter-in-law.

"Forgotten bride?" Lindsay said.

"Luke appeared to have forgotten you for the last few months, ever since the wedding date. We rather hoped the unfortunate incident would fade into the past."

"Mother!" Luke's voice was sharp with warning.

"Welcome to your new home, Lindsay," Catherine said flatly, her eyes showing no warmth.

Lindsay didn't know how to respond to such a blatant attempt to unnerve her. She had never met his mother when they'd frolicked on the beach. She hadn't remembered that until she faced Catherine. The visit to Lindsay's old apartment had not gone well. She nodded in reply and looked at Luke, realizing she still gripped his hand as if it were a lifeline. "Sorry," she murmured, slowly releasing her hold.

"Something to drink before dinner?" he asked.

Simmering tension permeated the room. Lindsay wondered if that was normal for this family. She rather doubted it. Undoubtedly she was the cause. So much for the hope she could ease things a bit while she visited. Did Luke have second thoughts already?

"Marabel told me dinner was at seven. I don't want to hold things up," Lindsay said.

"Marabel will do as she's told. If you wish for a drink, we have time," Luke said arrogantly.

"No, I'm fine."

"Mother?" Luke half turned to his mother, watching as she rose from the sofa and set her glass on the coffee table. "I'm ready for dinner," she said.

When she reached him, he offered his arm, then offered his other arm to Lindsay. She slipped her hand in the crook and turned to the dining room. Barely stifling a giggle, she wondered if they would play out this charade every night. At her flat, she ate in the kitchen more times than not. Of course, with only the baby to eat with, there had been no need for formality.

Luke sat at the head of the table, his mother to his left, Lindsay to his right. As soon as they were seated, Marabel entered carrying bowls of steaming soup.

"Luke told us you were a waitress when you married," Catherine said as she waited to be served. Her look indicated such a thing was almost beyond belief.

Lindsay looked across the table at the woman, instinctively knowing she was trying to rattle her. Tilting her chin slightly, she nodded, then smiled. "You could say that. Or you could say I was a student, since I was in school full time. Or that I was a purveyor of fine literature, since I also worked in a bookstore in the Strand," Lindsay said spiritedly. She would not be cowed by this woman. If Catherine Winters didn't like her son's choice of bride, she should have supported him against her father when Luke tried to make his own decisions. Instead, she'd aided and abetted her father in attempting to trap Luke into a loveless marriage for money and social standing.

"There's nothing wrong with any of those occupations, including being a waitress," Luke said firmly, glaring at his mother.

Lindsay dipped her spoon into the savory soup and took a sip. "This is delicious!" she said, in an attempt to turn the conversation to more amicable lines.

Marabel paused by the door to the kitchen. "Thank you for saying so, Mrs. Winters. I'll let Rachel know." With a triumphant smile she sailed through the door.

"How is Jonathan?" Luke asked his mother.

"About the same," Catherine responded, looking suddenly tired. "I sat with him this afternoon. He wanted me to read the paper to him, the business section, naturally. He talked about going into the office later this month. Luke, I'm so upset with the way he looks. Do you think another doctor could help?"

"Mother, we've had three doctors already. Each one has told us the same thing. Let's stick with the one we've got. Visit Jonathan as much as you can, but accept the fact he is not going to get better. I wish that weren't the case, but it is.''

Catherine sighed and dropped her gaze to her soup. Lindsay thought she saw the glimmer of tears in the older woman's eyes. Her heart ached in compassion. She knew what it was to be without a father. Catherine was lucky to have had hers for so many years.

"Did Ellie get settled in?" Luke asked.

"Ellie?" Catherine asked, looking up. Lindsay wondered if she'd imagined the tears. There were none showing now.

"Lindsay's little girl."

Catherine's gaze locked with Lindsay's. "So the baby was a girl. Is that what you used to trap my son?"

"I beg your pardon?" Lindsay asked, puzzled by the comment.

"You got pregnant to trap Luke into marriage?"

"Mother!"

Lindsay shook her head. "I'd say rather he married me in spite of my being pregnant, not because of it." She flicked a quick look at Luke, wondering what exactly he had told his family about his marriage.

"We've all wondered why he married you. You haven't played your cards very well up to this point. It's taken you more than four months to move in."

"I explained that Lindsay didn't feel comfortable moving in while I was in London," Luke said.

"You could have moved her in before you left," Catherine retaliated, her narrowed gaze never leaving Lindsay. Dislike was evident.

"Mo—"

"I can answer for myself, Luke. I would think you would be relieved I didn't marry your son for his money. Evidently his fiancée made no bones about that being her reason," Lindsay said firmly. She found it easy to stand up to this woman, probably because she truly didn't care what Catherine thought. She was in this masquerade solely to help out Luke.

"Jeannette would have suited him far better than you. She at least knows how to dress." With a disparaging look at Lindsay's dress, Catherine rendered judgment.

Lindsay laughed. It was that or cry. "Sorry if I'm not up to your standards. At home I don't even dress for dinner. I wear whatever I wore during the day. And usually eat in my kitchen. I don't have your fancy airs, Mrs. Winters. And I don't aspire to what you think is important. I have my daughter and I love her dearly. Together we are a family."

"And so far what you've seen of mine doesn't make you want to join right in, does it?" Luke broke in with a look at his mother.

Lindsay looked stricken.

"I'm sorry. I didn't mean to denigrate your family. But it seems so different from what my family was like. I'm glad I can make my own, that way I know it will suit me."

Catherine delicately pushed away her soup bowl and sat straighter in her chair. "I have given Luke every advantage. Even though his father deserted us, my father and I were able to see Luke lacked for nothing."

Lindsay nodded. "I don't know any of you. If you love your son, who am I to say that the manner in which you show that love is good or bad. I'm sure you hug him, kiss him, are interested in his dreams and goals. You probably have plenty to talk about when a stranger isn't in the room. Maybe I should take my meals in my room so as not to interrupt."

"That's enough!" Luke said, slapping a palm on the table. "Lindsay, you are my wife and will eat where I eat. If anyone takes a tray in her room, it will be my mother. But that won't be necessary. We have a man upstairs who is dying. I want his last days to be happy and will do all I can to insure that! So there will be no more sniping, no more insults and no more insinuations. Both of you will behave cordially to each other, or by God, I'll make you wish you had!"

Lindsay put down her spoon. She took a deep breath and

looked at Luke. "You know, Luke Winters, you mentioned you do not like to be dictated to. Well, we're evenly matched in that. I will not be dictated to, either. I'm here as a favor to you. If you don't like the way I'm handling things, I'll leave."

His hand snapped out to grip her wrist, holding hard. "Don't threaten me. I'll cut your funds off so fast you won't have enough money for breakfast."

Lindsay tugged but could not free her hand. She met his hard gaze. "I have some money in the bank and am bright enough to get a job that will support Ellie and me. I don't need your money."

"Then why are you here?"

"Because I never knew my grandfather, and even though I have no love for yours, I sympathize with your desire to make his last days happy. It's more than Will got."

"Who's Will?" Catherine asked.

"You're doing it for the money," Luke stated calmly, his eyes glittering as he held her gaze.

"No, Luke. I'm doing it for you."

He stared into her eyes until Lindsay felt light-headed. The rest of the dining room seemed to fade into a gray mist as she challenged his gaze. The truth of her words was evident to anyone who looked, but it wasn't her words that echoed in her senses, it was the feeling of coming home. The awareness of Luke as a man, a very virile and exciting man, that pounded through her. She had never felt so attuned to another, and a virtual stranger, at that. She and Will had been friends who married. The shattering awareness, the physical attraction and magnetic pull she felt around Luke had not been present with Will. It frightened her. It exhilarated her.

"Who's Will?" Catherine asked again.

"What do you get out of this?" Luke asked Lindsay, ignoring his mother.

"A chance to pay you back for helping me these last months. You enabled me to spend every minute with my

baby. It's been a precious time, and I would not have had
it had you not provided for me. I want to pay you back.''

Luke's gaze dropped to his hand banding her wrist.
Slowly he loosened his grip, sliding his palm down until it
covered the back of her hand. Lifting her hand, he bent and
kissed her palm lightly, set it down and released her.

"How romantic," Catherine said sarcastically.

Marabel pushed through the kitchen door at that moment,
platters of sliced beef and fish in each hand.

Lindsay hardly remembered what she ate that first night.
After the main course had been served, there was very little
conversation. She was anxious to go upstairs and check
Ellie. She still had to move her clothes to her own room
and find out from Luke what he wanted her to do during
the days when he was at work.

And there was still the meeting with Jonathan Balcomb
to get through.

In the end, the meeting with Luke's grandfather didn't
go as badly as Lindsay had feared. She worried about her
reaction to the man whose business tactics had caused
Will's death. But when Luke took her hand, threaded his
fingers through hers and led her into his grandfather's
room, she forgot about the anger that consumed her at the
thought of Jonathan Balcomb. She almost forgot her own
name.

Luke's hand held hers firmly, and his grip drew her attention like iron filings to a magnet. She liked the way his
hand clasped hers, like lovers, his strength tempered when
holding her. He was strong enough to stand between her
and the fear of the future, yet gentle enough to take the
very best care of her and her daughter. For a moment
Lindsay wished they were not playing make-believe. That
they had decided to make their marriage genuine and
weren't lying to an old man who lay dying.

Jonathan Balcomb had once been a tall, robust man, as
tall as Luke, Lindsay thought as she crept closer to the bed,
staying just a bit behind Luke. Compassion filled her as she

stared at the wasted figure lying so still in the huge bed. They should have found a smaller bed so he didn't look so lost, was her first thought.

"Jonathan?" Luke said softly. The nurse adjusted the lamp to provide more illumination without shining it directly into the eyes of the sick man.

When his lids flicked open, Lindsay knew where Luke had gotten his dark eyes. Even in his illness, Jonathan had the same piercing gaze.

"About time you got here, boy. Just because I turned the business over to you doesn't mean you can keep me in the dark about what's going on. And when you get into trouble, you'll need me to pull your bacon from the fire."

"Things are under control right now. I wanted you to meet Lindsay."

Jonathan turned his head and peered into the dim room. "Who?"

"My wife, Lindsay." Luke pulled her around before him and clamped his hands on her shoulders as if to hold her in place in case she decided to bolt.

"How do you do, Mr. Balcomb," she said softly.

"Ha! The waitress. You finally brought her home."

Lindsay winced. She disliked labels. "Actually, the college student, if you want to assign labels," she said firmly. "Why do the members of this family latch onto the waitressing job? I worked in a bookstore, too."

"Bet you haven't worked a day since you married Luke. Damn fool." Jonathan shifted his gaze to his grandson. "Told you then, I'll tell you again. Damn fool stunt."

"I'm content. I thought you'd be happy for me. You badgered me to marry for years. So I did."

"Jeannette Sullivan would have suited you better."

"No, she would have suited you and my mother better."

"So this young woman is the grand passion for which you threw over everything else?" Jonathan peered at Lindsay, his gaze searching.

"Drama seems to run in your family," Lindsay murmured, flicking a quick look at the nurse. The woman did not seem to feel that the visit was harming her patient.

"What's that? Speak up," Jonathan demanded.

"I'm happy to meet the rest of the family," she said a bit louder.

"I bet you are. But not as happy as landing Luke."

"He asked me to marry him, not the other way around," she said gently.

"How are you feeling today?" Luke asked, moving Lindsay to one side and drawing one of the chairs closer. "Feel up to talking about the Blackman deal?"

"Of course. This is temporary. I told your mother just today I expect to be in the office by the end of the month. Feel almost back to normal today. Right, nurse?"

"So you said, sir," she replied easily. "I'll leave you two gentlemen to talk. Ring the bell if you need anything."

"I'll leave, too," Lindsay said softly.

Luke turned to ask her to stay, but she was already halfway to the door. He hesitated, then turned to his grandfather, surprised by the shrewd look in his eyes.

"Quite a looker, that wife of yours. Has she come home to stay now, or is this a flying visit?" the old man asked.

"She's home to stay." For a moment Luke almost wished it were true.

"Send her to visit me tomorrow. I want to get to know this wife of yours."

"She'll stop by, I'm sure," Luke said, making a mental note to see if Lindsay would consider such a thing. At least she had not blurted out her anger at the old man for the death of her husband. Her first husband. For a moment Luke felt a strange sense of disorientation, almost jealousy. He had never met the dead man, but was envious of the love Lindsay felt for him. Would he find someone to love him that much one day?

Almost smiling, he turned his chair to better see his grandfather. He remembered the shocked look on his mother's face when Lindsay asked her if she hugged Luke or kissed him, knew his dreams and goals. Luke couldn't remember the last time he and his mother had talked about anything beyond the superficial topics of society.

He knew his mother cared deeply about her father and assumed she loved him. But she never overtly displayed any affection to anyone. And he wasn't sure he'd know what to do with it if she did.

"My Maggie was blond," Jonathan said reminiscently.

"Grandma?" Luke's memories were dim. She had died when he was a child. But he recalled gray hair, not blond.

"Yes, blond as gold, and pretty as a picture when the sun shone on it. It was as soft as velvet and always smelled so fresh. I loved to gather it in my hands and bury my face in it. God, I miss that woman. Never found another like her."

"We all missed her when she died," Luke said.

"Yes, I know Catherine was devastated. It wasn't too many years after that no-account husband left her. We're a pair, aren't we? Neither ever found another mate. There were plenty of men who wanted her. She was stubborn, just like you. I wish she'd found someone. You love that girl, Luke?" he asked sharply.

"Why else would I defy you to marry her?" he responded, sidestepping the issue.

"I hope you find the same happiness me and your grandmother had. Lying here day after day gets a man to thinking." Jonathan trailed off. The seconds ticked by. Then he seemed to remember Luke was in the room. "Tell me about this deal you've got cooking with Blackman. You have to watch him, he is a shifty bastard."

Luke sat with his grandfather until the old man drifted to sleep. Sometimes when Jonathan talked on and on about deals he'd completed in the past, Luke's mind wandered. Tonight he recalled the conversation at dinner and the reaction he'd felt when Lindsay told her reason for consenting to participate in his deception—for him. It had been years since anyone had done something for him. Usually people wanted something from him. He had money, so friends never hesitated to ask for loans, which were never repaid. He had power in the industry and took calls every day from people who wanted favors, which they usually did not return. How long had it been since someone had done something for him? Just for his asking?

He couldn't figure Lindsay out. She didn't follow the normal trend of the young women he knew. She wasn't clothes-conscious. Didn't seem to care much for money. And came across as independent as hell—wanting to do things her way, for herself. Maybe it was a good idea to go outside his circle of friends to find someone to marry. His marriage was temporary. When it was time, Lindsay would get her annulment and go on her way. Once that happened, if he wanted a wife, he'd have to start looking again.

He shook his head and brought his attention to what his grandfather was saying. Before long, Jonathan trailed off, his eyes closing.

Luke crossed to the lamp and turned it low. He covered the man who had been like a father to him, regret at the wasting of such a vital life constantly with him. In less than three months, the once tall and robust man he'd known all his life had been reduced to a thin, frail, desperately ill individual. The worst part was knowing there was nothing he could do to stop the inevitable.

Luke rubbed his eyes. Despite the brief nap at Lindsay's that afternoon, he was dead tired. He'd go to bed now. But if his grandfather woke in the middle of the night and wanted to talk, he'd get up to sit with him. Time was too short to waste on sleeping when he could spend it with the old man.

Light spilled into the hall from the nursery. Luke veered from his room to the open doorway and looked in. He had not yet seen Lindsay's baby. The soft glow of the lamp illuminated the room. Lindsay sat rocking gently, reading a book. In the crib, resting on her stomach with her bottom up in the air, lay a tiny child. Quietly Luke entered. He nodded to Lindsay but moved directly to the crib. Gazing down at the little girl sleeping there, he smiled. Most of what he saw was covered by a blanket. Only a mop of baby-fine brown curls and one pink cheek showed. Her lashes were long and lay on her chubby cheeks like dark shadows. Her tiny hand fisted near her mouth. He wondered if she sucked her thumb.

"She's very pretty," he said softly.

"She won't wake up," Lindsay said in a normal tone. Rising from the rocker, she put down the book and went to stand beside him. "I was worried she might be uneasy in a new house, but she has her blanket and her teddy bear. She learned to sleep through the night a couple of months ago, so I expect her to do so tonight." She gazed at Ellie for a moment, then turned to Luke.

"This room is great, by the way. Thank you."

"Thank you for coming, Lindsay. It helped. Tonight Jonathan referred to my grandmother for the first time since she died. I don't ever remember him talking about her. He loved her."

"He must miss her every day."

"Jonathan is the only father I've known. Mine left shortly before I was born."

"Then you must love him a lot."

"I can't believe he's dying. I'll miss him."

Lindsay slipped her hand into his and squeezed it for comfort. "But you had him a long time. Maybe not as long as you wanted, but you will have good memories, right? And you'll know you pleased him in the end. We'll pretend that this is the best marriage in the world, and he'll die thinking his grandson is happy. That's probably all he wants."

Luke rested their hands on the side of the crib and stared at the baby for a long time. She was adorable. Suddenly he wanted to see her awake, see what color her eyes were. Gray like her mother's? Did her smile resemble Lindsay's?

Could she roll over yet? Sit up? He had no idea what to expect from a baby. But he wouldn't mind learning.

Slowly he became aware of the woman standing quietly beside him. She came to his chin. If he leaned over to kiss her, he wouldn't have to lean far. His hand tightened around hers. She was slender yet curved in the right places. Rubbing his thumb gently over the satiny skin of her hand, he wondered if she were that warm and soft all over. He glanced down.

"Where's the wedding ring I bought?" he asked, noticing the bare finger.

"It was too big once I stopped retaining water. It kept falling off." Slowly she drew a chain from beneath her dress. There at the end glittered the gold ring he'd hastily purchased for their wedding.

"You could have had it sized," he said, fingering it gently. It was still warm from being pressed against her body.

"I guess I could have. But I didn't really consider this a true marriage."

"It's as legal as they get," he murmured, sliding the ring back and forth on the chain.

Lindsay shrugged, mesmerized by his hand holding hers, the other rubbing the ring against the chain—the symbol of their marriage.

While she had not had the ring sized, she still wore it. Out of loyalty? Luke did not care to ask why. It was enough that she'd worn it.

"Luke."

"Yes?" He stopped playing with the ring. "Give me the ring and I'll take care of it," he said.

"Marabel put my things in your room," Lindsay blurted.

"So?" He unfastened the chain and slid the ring into his palm.

"So where am I supposed to sleep?"

Looking up, he caught her wary gaze. Slowly he smiled. "With your husband, of course. Come with me."

CHAPTER FOUR

"YOU can't be serious!" she said two seconds later when Luke pulled her into his room. Lindsay's blood heated at the mere thought. She took in his wide shoulders, his dark hair, the way his eyes crinkled at the corners when he smiled. And her heart raced. Share a room with this man?

"We're married." Humor lurked in his eyes. "Have been for more than four months."

Lindsay swallowed, conscious of how close he stood, of the warmth from his body, which seemed to encircle her, captivate her. She could smell his after-shave and the slight tang of his unique masculine scent. A strange excitement started to build deep inside. She hadn't felt this giddy since those long-ago days at the beach.

"Luke." She took a step back, as if distance could alter things. "Think about this. We don't know each other. We haven't seen each other since we were teenagers. We've scarcely been together for more than a couple of hours all told. And this isn't a real marriage."

"It's real."

"I know it's legal, you made sure of that. But we're just pretending for your grandfather's sake. It's not a *real* marriage." She pressed her hand against her stomach as if to still the fluttering butterflies. He couldn't really want to sleep with her—could he?

"Do you ever wish it were?" he asked, stepping closer, crowding her.

Almost in panic, Lindsay stepped back until she came up against the cool wood of his bedroom door. Trapped, she frantically sought a rational answer. Even as her mind spun, a small part wondered what it would be like to have him kiss her, to hold her tightly. Would his hands be hard or soft, tender or demanding? Would his lips be warm or cool? She suspected his body would feel strong and hard—feeding the suddenly feminine feelings that flooded her. Conscious of the difference between them, how they would complement each other, softness to strength, female to male, she pushed against the door, watching him warily.

"Luke, no."

"Relax, Lindsay, I'm not going to pounce on you just because we are behind closed doors."

She swallowed. "Then step back."

He smiled, devilish lights dancing in his eyes. "Afraid?" he asked softly, not moving a muscle.

Instantly she knew she was not. He would never intentionally hurt her. While ruthless in many areas, she'd seen him tolerate his mother when she exasperated him beyond belief. And he loved his grandfather, despite the machinations the old man had tried. Luke was too much a man to ever harm someone smaller than he.

"No, I'm not afraid." Not of him. But Lindsay was beginning to fear the feelings that grew inside her. Temptation exploded when he looked at her with that intimate smile. Her fingers itched to trace that hard jaw, to brush back his dark hair and test its texture. Her body yearned to feel the excitement of being held, of being pressed against a masculine body. Her lips almost ached with longing for his touch.

Feeling foolish and infatuated, she looked away, her gaze landing on the bed. Heat flushed her cheeks.

"We can't sleep together," she repeated almost desperately. Saying it did nothing to dispel the images that danced before her of the two of them kissing, holding each other, tangled in the sheets.

He chuckled and turned away, shrugging out of his suit jacket. "Then where do you suggest we sleep?" He opened the large closet and slipped the jacket on a hanger. He yanked down his tie and hung it on a rack to the left. As he began to unbutton his shirt, he turned and looked at her.

Mesmerized, Lindsay remained where he'd left her. Surely he wasn't planning to undress in front of her? With effort she moved her gaze from the open shirt to his eyes.

"This house has a lot of rooms. Just point me in the direction of an empty one."

"And have everyone know by morning that we are not sleeping together? I don't think that will further our deception for Jonathan."

She swallowed as he pulled the shirt from his trousers and tossed it on a nearby chair. His shoulders were broad and lightly muscled, his chest firm and sculpted. He looked as if he worked with his hands rather than his head. Clenching her hands into fists, Lindsay crossed her arms across her chest and moved away from the door, away from the tantalizing display of masculine perfection. Daydreams were fine for teenagers, but she was a mother, a widow and—and the wife of the man now undressing!

"I don't know what to suggest. But I am—"

"Lindsay."

"What?" She spun around and met his eyes.

"Look at the size of that bed. We can sleep in it and never even know the other person is in it. I didn't bring you here for seduction. Even I have a little more finesse than that. But I told you how important this charade is to me. I don't want to end it before it even begins. I promise I won't touch you."

"Well." She bit her lip, undecided. Hadn't she done enough? She had agreed to this sham of a marriage, agreed today to pretend they were in love to help make his grandfather's last days happier.

"Unless you want me to, of course," he murmured softly.

And that was the problem. Part of her did want him to touch her. It had been so long since she'd been held, kissed, made love to. She hadn't minded so much when it was just

Ellie. But these last few hours had shown her she was sus-
ceptible to a man's charm. To a man's pull of attraction.
And she hardly knew him!

"No," she said, wondering if that was strictly true.

Luke held her eye for a moment longer, then nodded. He
took a pullover from the chest of drawers and yanked it on.
"I have work in the study. I'll be up in a couple of hours.
Go to bed, Lindsay, and fall asleep before I show up. You'll
never know I'm there."

"I could sleep on the floor," she offered.

"Whatever. The bed's big enough. Did you get the baby
monitor?"

"The what?"

He frowned. "I set up a baby monitor. Did you get the
receiver?"

She shook her head.

"Come on." He led the way to the nursery. A soft glow
emanated from the small light on the wall. He crossed to
the dresser, picked up a small plastic receiver, flipped a
switch and handed it to her.

"See the unit on the wall near the crib?"

She nodded.

"It'll pick up noise in this room. If your baby awakens
in the night, you can hear her through the receiver." He
pointed to the device in her hand. "The range is quite good.
You can hear her all over the house and yard."

Lindsay was touched that he'd thought about how she'd
fret being so far from the baby and had taken steps to insure
she would be free to wander around and yet know instantly
when Ellie awoke. "Thank you, Luke."

"Good night, Lindsay."

She watched him leave and sighed softly, trying to define
her feelings for him. Since he'd walked into the café, her
behavior had been in question. She still had trouble believing she accepted his original proposal and married him.
Though she wondered how she could have managed Ellie's
birth without his generous allowance. Was it only that af-

ternoon that he'd shown up and asked her to move into his house for the next few weeks? So much that had transpired since then, it seemed much longer. But less than twelve hours ago she had been eating lunch with her daughter propped up near her and planning to go to the park after Ellie's nap. Now she was firmly ensconced in Luke's house pretending to be his loving wife, had met his mother and grandfather and would be sharing Luke's bedroom. Gripping the receiver, she headed to the master bedroom feeling a bit like a condemned prisoner going to her doom.

A half hour later, Lindsay had soaked in a warm bath and changed for bed, donning a long T-shirt. At least she couldn't be accused of trying to seduce her husband. Not that she had any sleepwear that would accomplish that. She liked the feel of cotton against her skin. Slipping between the covers of her makeshift bed, she tried to find a comfortable position. The pile of blankets weren't as comfortable as a real mattress, but she couldn't bring herself to climb into Luke's bed. She knew he'd be a gentleman, he'd said so, and he was a man of his word. But it felt too strange, too tempting. She'd be better off on the floor.

Slowly her eyes closed as sleep claimed her. Tomorrow she'd see about getting some sort of air mattress or something.

When Lindsay awoke the next morning, she was alone in the bedroom. Comfy and warm—in Luke's bed!

Her eyes flew open. She was in his bed? How? She distinctly remembered making a bed on the floor near the window. Turning, she spotted the tumble of blankets. Heat washed through her. Had she stumbled into the bed during the night? Or had Luke picked her up and placed her in it?

For a moment she wondered if Luke had come to bed. Or had he slept elsewhere? The indentation in the pillow next to hers showed he'd slept there. She stretched out her hand, and her fingers caressed the cool sheets. He'd obviously left quite a while ago. Sighing softly, for a moment she almost resented the fact he'd been right. She had not known they were sharing a bed. She couldn't believe she'd slept through the process of getting into his bed. What if Ellie had cried during the night. Would she have slept through that?

Lindsay quickly showered and dressed. Ellie would be awake soon, and she didn't want the baby to inconvenience anyone. But she wasn't sure how she would face Luke this morning. Quickly picking up the blankets, she folded them and replaced them in the closet where she'd found them. If they were to perpetuate this deception, she didn't want Marabel or anyone to know she'd made a bed on the floor.

Just as Lindsay slipped into her shoes, she heard her daughter's familiar cries transmitted through the receiver. Grabbing the device, Lindsay hurried toward Ellie's room.

A half hour later the two of them headed down the big stairs. Reaching the ground floor, Lindsay saw Luke finishing his breakfast at the dining table. Swallowing hard with embarrassment, she stepped into the dining room.

"Good morning," she said.

He looked up and smiled. "Good morning." He rose and came around the table, holding her gaze until he reached her. Leaning over, he kissed her. Before she could say a word, he then kissed the baby's cheek.

Ellie's head wobbled a bit, but she pulled back from her mother's shoulder and eyed the man standing so close, her eyes wide and solemn.

"May I?" He reached out and took the child, holding her awkwardly.

Lindsay found it impossible to stop her grin. Luke looked even bigger than normal holding the infant. Yet there was something strongly appealing about such a strong masculine man cuddling a small child. Ellie didn't seem to mind his uncertainty. Her gaze never wavered from his face. She didn't fuss or cry, but seemed content in his large hands. Just then Marabel entered with a fresh pot of tea.

"Good morning, missus," the housekeeper said with a huge grin. "How's the baby today?"

"She slept fine. At least I didn't hear her in the night." She looked at Luke in confusion. How soundly had she slept last night?

"I checked on her before I came to bed. She was sleeping soundly," he said. "Marabel, can you find the baby carrier?"

"Luke, I don't want to interrupt your breakfast," Lindsay protested.

"I'd like my two girls to share breakfast with me. Wouldn't you like that, Ellie?" he asked, but his eyes remained on Lindsay.

"Don't say I didn't warn you if she starts fussing," she murmured, still flustered by his kiss. As kisses went, it had been brief, almost impersonal. But it had surprised her, and flooded her with long-forgotten delight. Following him to the table, she licked her lips—she could almost feel his lips against hers. Did she taste him? Or was her imagination working overtime?

She cleared her throat as she sat down, flicking a nervous glance around the empty room, then at Luke. "I, uh, see we ended up sharing the bed after all."

He nodded, his eyes holding hers. "And nothing happened, right?"

"I guess not."

"It has to be more comfortable than the floor."

"Here we go," Marabel said as she entered carrying the padded baby carrier. Setting it beside Ellie, she nodded as if in satisfaction.

"What do you have planned for today?" Luke asked when the baby had been firmly tucked into the carrier.

"Is there something you want me to do?" she asked, anxious to do what she could to help him out.

"No. I had Hedley pick you up yesterday to get your things, but I didn't think about your car. He can drive you back today if you like so you can pick it up."

"I don't have a car," she said, slowly spreading jam on a piece of toast.

"No car?"

Lindsay glanced up at his tone. "No. Will and I only had one car, and it was wrecked in the accident. I didn't want to spend the insurance money on another one. I took the bus to work and school. Once Ellie was born, I knew I'd need money to delay as long as possible the need to return to work."

"I'll see about getting you a car. In the meantime, if you need to go anywhere, ask Hedley, he'll take you."

"I don't need a car, Luke. For heaven's sake, I'm only here for—" She stopped, thinking how awful to remind him she would leave when his grandfather died. "For a while."

"I'll buy you a car, and you can take it with you when you go," he said.

She put down the spoon and turned to look at him. "Luke, you can't buy me a car!"

He shrugged. "Why not? You're my wife."

Marabel bustled in from the kitchen at that moment, and Lindsay fell into a fuming silence. Money didn't buy everything. She didn't need him to buy her a car. It was bad enough taking the allowance he provided. Now that she'd seen his family, she thought that Luke could have found another way to demonstrate to his grandfather he wouldn't be manipulated. A hint of regret that she'd agreed to the marriage crept in. Was she being unfair to him?

"I brought you eggs and sausage," Marabel said, placing the plate before Lindsay. "The tea's hot. Luke, pass her the milk. Is there anything else you'd like?"

Lindsay shook her head, anxious for Marabel to leave so she could respond to Luke's last comment.

"It's a temporary marriage," she whispered when the door closed behind the housekeeper. "I can use Hedley, if he's available. I know you get first call."

"Hedley isn't my chauffeur, he's Jonathan's. But I am putting him up while Jonathan's staying here. Hedley has very little to do now that Jonathan's so ill. He'll be around if you want to go anywhere. It'll give him something to do to earn his keep.''

"Oh.''

Luke looked up. ''You're my wife. You are entitled to anything I have, and that certainly includes the services of the household staff.''

"Good morning, Luke.'' Catherine Winters trailed into the dining room dressed in a lavender satin robe. She paused near an empty chair and looked at Ellie's carrier sitting in the middle of the table.

Meeting Lindsay's gaze, she smiled politely. ''Your baby's very pretty,'' she said stiffly.

"Thank you. Her name's Ellie,'' Lindsay replied.

Catherine looked as if she wanted to say something else, but merely nodded regally and waited while Luke pulled out her chair. Once she was seated, she turned to her son.

"I will need Hedley to run some errands for me today, Luke. Would you let him know?''

"If Lindsay doesn't need him,'' Luke said as he sat at the head of the table and folded his paper.

"Of course, your wife must always come first,'' Catherine said sarcastically, darting a hard look at Lindsay.

"Mother.'' Luke's tone warned of dire consequences should she continue along that line.

Making a snap decision, Lindsay smiled at Luke and Catherine. ''Actually, I do need Hedley this morning. We'll be back after lunch in time for Ellie's nap. He would be available all afternoon if that would suit you.'' She held Catherine's gaze, not giving an inch. If Luke wanted to establish a hierarchy in his home, far be it from her to deny him the pleasure. Besides, Catherine's attitude rubbed her the wrong way. Served her right to have to wait a while.

Catherine's lips tightened, but she nodded. ''That would be fine.''

Lindsay escaped the dining room as soon as she finished eating, using the excuse of needing to dress the baby for their errands. Grimly she marched to the nursery. Her idea of using Hedley to drive her this morning had been born of desperation. She did not want to remain in the house once Luke left for work. It would be too much of a strain fending off his mother's sly comments and trying to maintain their facade before Marabel. She'd take the baby to the park, maybe visit Jack at the café and talk to him while getting something to eat before returning home in the afternoon. The old man loved Ellie, and Lindsay was always glad to see him.

Ellie squirmed in Lindsay's arms when they returned to Luke's home that afternoon. She had been fretful all morning, missing her normal nap, and was just warming up to a good cry. Lindsay would be glad when she went to sleep and gave her a few hours of rest!

"Did you have a nice time in the park?" Marabel asked when she opened the door. Ellie swiveled her head at the housekeeper. She stuck her thumb in her mouth and looked as if she'd start to cry. Lindsay jiggled her gently and nodded.

"We did, but it's past time she slept, and am I glad! I don't know how I'll cope when she's walking and into everything."

"Children can sure run a person ragged. And they need less sleep as they get older. Doesn't seem fair somehow," Marabel agreed.

Lindsay smiled at her daughter, love swelling in her heart. She would grow up so fast. Did Catherine ever remember when Luke was so small? She shook her head at the wayward thought. She didn't think Catherine ever thought of anything but herself. Smiling at Marabel, she climbed the stairs.

"We'll tuck you up and let you sleep, baby girl. When you wake up, we can go out into the garden and explore, would you like that?" Lindsay asked as she changed Ellie's diapers.

"Excuse me, Mrs. Winters."

Lindsay turned. The nurse stood in the doorway.

"Yes?" She wasn't used to being called Mrs. Winters.

"Mr. Balcomb would like to see you and the baby, if you can spare a couple of minutes."

"I was going to put her to sleep. She's a bit fussy."

"I understand, but I don't think it will bother him. And his sleeping schedule is even more erratic than a young baby's. Please?"

Slowly Lindsay nodded, wishing Luke were home. She didn't want to visit Jonathan Balcomb alone.

When Lindsay paused in the doorway, she saw the old man half sitting, leaning on one arm as he stared eagerly at the child she held. The nurse stepped aside and murmured she'd be back soon.

"You wanted to see us?" Lindsay said, crossing slowly to the edge of his bed.

"Your daughter?" Jonathan asked hoarsely, his eyes never leaving Ellie.

Lindsay nodded. She swallowed hard. Hadn't Luke told his grandfather about Ellie?

Jonathan lay back heavily. "I didn't know there was a child. He never told me. Damnation, Luke should have told me!"

"I'll put her down for her nap," Lindsay said, turning to leave.

"Wait. It's not every day a man meets a new grandchild. What's her name?"

Lindsay opened her mouth to tell him Ellie was not Luke's child, then closed it when she saw the gleam of excitement in the old man's eyes. Light color tinged his cheeks, and he looked better than last night.

"Her name is Ellie."

"No wonder he married you instead of Jeannette. Hello, Ellie," Jonathan said. "Never mentioned the baby, though. Should have. I like babies."

The baby stopped fussing and turned her head to the sound of his rusty voice.

"You didn't play my grandson false, now did you?" he snapped, glaring at Lindsay.

She tilted her chin and stared back, refusing to be intimidated yet unsure how Luke wanted her to handle this. "Ellie's my husband's child," she said.

"Ah." A smile of satisfaction filled Jonathan's face. "Cute thing. How old is she?"

"Almost four months."

"Not too big for her age, is she? Luke's a big man."

Lindsay shrugged. She turned Ellie so Jonathan could see her better.

"You watch her closely. Make sure Marabel and the others clear up the house. Too many things around this place aren't suitable for a baby. I wouldn't want her to get hurt."

Lindsay stared at him for a moment, wishing he'd felt as strongly about the equipment in his company. Will had been more than hurt. She nodded, knowing they wouldn't be here long enough for Ellie to get into mischief. A pang of regret pierced her. Lindsay had been furious at the cause of her husband's death, but wishing harm to this ailing old man wouldn't bring Will back. She had to remember that.

"I will," she said coolly. She turned and left the room.

Luke reached the top of the stairs and started toward his grandfather's room just as Nurse Spencer came into the hall and closed the door behind her.

"Is he sleeping?"

"Oh, you startled me, sir. Yes, he just dropped off."

"How's he doing today?"

"About the same. Your daughter's visit cheered him up," the nurse said. "I thought I'd take a walk around the garden."

"The weather is beautiful today," Luke said carefully, stunned by what the nurse said. He turned and headed toward the other end of the hall. His daughter, hmm? Why had Lindsay taken Ellie in to see Jonathan? Immediately Luke considered the various angles to the situation. Was she holding out for more money? He'd been surprised she had not angled for more when he proposed to set up a trust fund for her and Ellie. Maybe she felt it would be more lucrative to worm her way into the old man's affections and get a bigger piece of the pie.

Luke pushed open the door to the nursery. Ellie lay fast asleep in her crib. The magazine Lindsay had been reading last night was still facedown on the rocking chair.

He crossed the hall to their room. Last night he'd stayed away as long as he could, finally giving in when he dozed off in the study. He'd been surprised when he'd opened the door to find the bed empty. He thought she'd sought another room until he'd spied the bundle beneath the window. She'd been fast asleep. Torn between exasperation and amusement, he'd picked her up and deposited her on the bed. It was huge, large enough for each to ignore the other beneath the covers.

So he had thought. But he had not been able to ignore Lindsay. Her blond curls had softly framed her face like old gold in the faint illumination. She had looked young and trusting lying so peacefully in his bed—even though he had wondered what she'd say or do if she awoke.

The feelings he'd experienced waking up beside her had been unexpected. He rarely spent the night, even when involved with someone. For a long moment, he wanted to pull her into his arms and kiss her. He blasted his younger self for turning away from her when they'd been kids. She was even more beautiful now than that pretty girl at the beach.

Instead, he'd calmly risen and dressed for the day. But he had a kiss in the dining room.

Their room empty, Luke walked down the hall, almost smiling in memory of her surprise at that kiss. He'd heard Marabel coming and wanted to perpetuate the myth of a happy marriage. But the act backfired. Now he wondered what it would be like to kiss Lindsay because they both wanted it, not for show. She was soft and sweet, and yet from time to time she flared up at him. Hidden passion could sometimes be the strongest. Would she be passionate with the right man? Had she been so with her husband?

Frowning at the trend of his thoughts, Luke ran down the stairs. He only wanted to convince his grandfather he was happy so the old man could die peacefully. What went on in Lindsay's life before yesterday didn't matter.

Though how anyone could expect them to have a happy marriage after the manner of their wedding was beyond him. Anyone who knew him knew he was skeptical on the subject. His experience with women didn't lend itself to believing in love and happy ever after. The only woman he thought he'd cared for had proved she could be bought more easily than fall in love. His mother had played the role of abandoned wife for years, when in fact she'd left her husband for the money her father's life-style offered. And Luke had seen nothing over the years to show him any woman was different.

Still, as long as he could convince his grandfather that he and Lindsay had a happy marriage, that was all that mattered.

Dammit, where was she? She wouldn't have gone far with Ellie upstairs napping. He glanced into the living room in passing, heading for the back of the house. Hearing voices in the kitchen, he pushed open the door and stopped.

Lindsay stood at the counter, rolling out some kind of dough. She chatted away with Rachel and Marabel as if they were all old friends.

"Lindsay?" Luke said.

She spun around, her eyes wide at seeing him. "Hi, Luke. What are you doing home so early?" Wiping her hands on the towel beside the dough, she waited to hear what he had to say.

"I came home to see Jonathan. He's sleeping right now. What are you doing?"

"Making an apple pie. Do you like them?"

"Yes. Can't Rachel?" He flicked a quick glance at the cook.

"I'm sure she can, but this is my own recipe. I'll be finished in a few minutes."

"Join me in the study when you're finished."

When Lindsay stepped into the study a short time later, Luke stood by the window, gazing out across the garden. He'd discarded his suit jacket, and the breadth of his shoulders was emphasized by the pristine dress shirt. She remembered those shoulders from yesterday, when he'd discarded his shirt. Rubbing her hands along the side of her legs, she tried a smile.

"You wanted to see me?" Lindsay asked.

He turned and nodded. "Have a seat."

She glanced at the small sofa near the fireplace and at the chairs near the desk. She chose the sofa.

Luke moved to stand near the empty fireplace, struck once again by how pretty she looked, and how different from the day he'd married her.

"Did you lose a lot of weight?" he asked.

She nodded. "Of course, I was pregnant when you met me, and retaining water. Once Ellie was born, I lost the water and most of the extra pounds from being pregnant." She raised her eyebrows. "Is something wrong?"

"No. In the future, use the bed. You may have lost weight, but it is hard to pick up a sleeping woman from the floor."

Lindsay blushed and nodded, looking away as embarrassment claimed her.

"I understand you took Ellie in to see my grandfather," he said.

"What?" She looked at him, then nodded. "The nurse said he asked for me, and to see the baby. Did you tell him Ellie was his? He seems to think he's her great-grandfather. Even ordered me to make the house baby-proof."

Luke made a mental note to make sure Marabel did what was necessary. "So you told him Ellie was mine?"

Lindsay looked puzzled, shaking her head slowly, then her expression cleared. "Nurse Spencer, I presume, is the source of all this?"

"She mentioned it."

"Actually I told your grandfather that Ellie was my husband's child. I wasn't sure what story you wanted concocted about her, so I did my best."

Luke turned one of the chairs from the desk, straddled it and rested his hands on the back. "I'm not in the habit of concocting stories."

She shrugged. "You are trying to pass our marriage off as a real and loving one. How do I know what you are in the habit of doing? Besides, your grandfather seemed very happy at the thought that Ellie might be yours."

Luke stared at her, trying to decide whether to perpetuate this latest lie or set the record straight. He sighed. He loved his grandfather, owed him loyalty and respect for all he'd done for him over the years. But it was hard to lie to the man, even for the sake of bringing happiness to his final days.

"Is that the end of the inquisition?" she asked quietly.

"A few friendly questions hardly comprise an inquisition," Luke drawled, his gaze firmly on her face.

"Your friendly technique needs work."

He shrugged. "There's a charity ball on Friday. We've been invited to attend. I usually support the organization, so I'd like us to go."

"Us?" Lindsay sat up at that.

"Any reason we can't?"

"There are probably a dozen, starting with I don't have anything suitable to wear, going on to who would mind Ellie, and then there's the fact I've never been to one of those fancy balls and don't have a clue how to behave."

"Then, sweetheart, you've come to the right place. Organization is one of my skills. You can go shopping with Mother tomorrow and find a dress. Marabel will be delighted to watch Ellie, not that she'll need any special care.

The ball doesn't start until eight. Ellie will be in bed by then. And there is nothing to do at the ball but enjoy yourself. And show everyone how much you adore me.''

"I knew there'd be a catch.''

CHAPTER FIVE

"MAYBE we should get some practice in," he suggested smoothly.

"Practice?" Lindsay grew wary at the devilish light in his eye. For a moment she remembered the older boy on the beach. What was he up to?

"If pretending to be a loving wife is so difficult, we could practice."

"I can wing it at the ball," she replied quickly, her imagination already racing with wild images. She could sit in his lap after dinner, nibbling kisses against his jaw. Or they could stroll in the garden and find a secluded arbor where he could kiss her until her toes curled. And there was always the big bed upstairs that they'd shared last night. Lindsay swallowed hard. She had to get those tumbling pictures out of her head!

"If you are sure."

She saw the amusement in his eyes and frowned. "Should we even be going with your grandfather so ill?"

The amusement vanished. "I'm trying to keep things as normal as possible, except for spending more time at home than usual. He isn't convinced he's dying," Luke said slowly.

"And is he? Couldn't he get well?"

"No, Lindsay, he won't get well. And he won't live many more weeks. According to the doctors, he'll get gradually weaker and weaker until he can no longer eat properly. He'll lapse into a coma, and then it will just be a matter of days or even hours until he's gone."

"I'm sorry."

Luke pushed away from the chair and spun it around.

81

Walking to the window, he looked out onto the garden. It was summer, late January, and everything was in full bloom. He hated the thought his grandfather wouldn't see next summer's blossoms. Of all the holidays he'd miss. Of the hole he'd leave in his life.

"Yes, well, I'm sorry, too. He's the only father I've known. He can be hard to deal with, but—" Clenching his hands into fists, Luke fought the wave of despair that came whenever he thought of losing Jonathan.

Lindsay rose swiftly and crossed the room to stand beside Luke. Her hand touched his arm tentatively. She squeezed gently. "It's never easy to lose a loved one. But, Luke, in one small way you're lucky. You know this time is fleeting. Take the hours you have and make them count. I thought Will and I had forever. Then one day in an instant he was gone. Do you know he never even knew I was pregnant? I wish I had had a few weeks, knowing he would die, to tell him how much being married to him meant, to tell him about our baby. Take this time with your grandfather and be grateful you have it. So many people lose loved ones suddenly and unexpectedly and have to live all the rest of their lives knowing there were things they wished they'd said."

He looked at her, seeing the tears in her eyes, the earnestness of her expression. Encircling her shoulders, he drew her near, looked out the window.

"Tell me about your husband, Lindsay. About growing up after that last summer at the beach. I know very little about you except you were a pest at the beach. An enchanting pest, sometimes. We saw each other for five summers. That's not a lot of time, is it?"

She shrugged but didn't move away from his embrace. "Will and I were both orphans who met at a concert. In the crowded lobby, no less, can you believe it? Neither one of us had a date that night, so when he invited me out for coffee when the concert ended, I went. I remember him as always being so much fun. We laughed all the time. And did crazy things people do when they're young." For a moment she was silent. The memories threatened to engulf her. Swallowing hard, she smiled. They had been so young and a bit naive in retrospect.

"Like what?" He wanted to know more about this woman who had agreed to help him one night. What memories did she cherish?

"Will loved kites. We designed them and then constructed them. When we'd fly them in the park, people would stop and talk to us. Half the time Will gave the kite to someone who admired it. Which was fine, that meant we could make more. Sometimes he'd fly them at the beach. We always drew a crowd, and by the end of the day had made new friends. We'd stay up late, and be so tired in the mornings we could hardly get out of bed to go to work."

"I know you are originally from Sydney. Did your aunt live here, too?"

"Yes. My aunt lived over near The Rocks. We had a nice flat there. She really didn't want to be responsible for a child. She'd never married, didn't seem the maternal type. As soon as I was old enough to be on my own she took off for Tasmania. I often wonder why we couldn't have gone there even when I was a child. But it was her dream, and she had to live it her way, I guess."

"And your dreams?"

"Some of them died when Will did. I'll make new ones in time, but for now I have my baby, and…"

"And?" Luke turned her slightly so he could look into her face.

Mischievously she grinned. "And a demanding husband and an irate mother-in-law. And I'm part of a huge deception. Not the stuff of dreams, but it sure is interesting."

Luke smiled slowly. Just as slowly he lowered his head until his breath brushed across her cheeks. He could see Lindsay's eyes widen slightly as she realized his intent. But she didn't move, didn't turn away.

Closing his mouth over hers, he pushed against her until

she backed to the windowsill, then stepped closer until he felt her body against his. He reached out to hold her. Moving persuasively, he coaxed a response from her. The kiss lasted endless moments. Pushing for more, he teased her with his tongue on her lips until she opened to him. For a long moment, Luke felt as if he'd come home.

"Well, really, couldn't that be better done in private?" Catherine's voice splashed across them like ice water.

Lindsay jerked, but Luke slowly released her, his eyes watching her warily.

"Do you need something, Mother?" Luke asked as he turned around.

"I would expect a bit of decorum in the house. What if Marabel walked in?" Catherine asked, outraged. She closed the door behind her and advanced across the carpet, her eyes flashing.

"What if she did? She works for me. Do you think she would find it shocking that a man would kiss his wife?"

Catherine raised her nose delicately. "I hardly think the study is the place for that sort of thing."

"And I think any place is the place, if it suits me," Luke said calmly. "Did you want something?"

"My father is awake and wondering if you were home yet," she said stiffly.

"I went up to see him when I first arrived. He was napping."

"He's awake now."

"Then I'll go right up." Luke looked at Lindsay. "You all right?"

Lindsay nodded, avoiding his eyes and Catherine's. She was getting good at deception. She had never felt like this before and wasn't sure *all right* described it. Her heart raced, her skin tingled, her blood pounded through her and her knees were wobbly. All from a single kiss.

Trying a smile, she pushed away from the window, lest she be left behind with Catherine. "I'll go check on my pie," she said breathlessly. Great, even her voice was affected.

"What pie?" Catherine asked sharply.

"I'm baking an apple pie for dessert," Lindsay said as she reached the door. She almost ran down the hall, anxious to escape Catherine and Luke. And her own emotions, which threatened to overwhelm her because of a single kiss.

Doing her best during the afternoon to avoid her husband and his mother, Lindsay stayed in the kitchen until the pie was a golden brown. She took it from the oven and set it proudly on the counter, relieved it had turned out perfect. She heard Ellie on the monitor a short time later. She fed the baby then took her into the garden and settled her in the dappled shade of a tall gum tree. The little girl's roaming gaze paused at the array of colorful flowers, and she gazed at the blossoms for long moments. She squirmed around on her blanket, as if trying to turn over. Lindsay scooped her up and, laughing, gently swung her around.

"Come on, baby, let Mama show you how to smell the roses. Watch for bees."

Ellie grabbed at a rose and pulled back her hand in surprise as a fist full of petals drifted down.

"Eye-hand coordination needs a bit of work yet, sweetie," Lindsay murmured, snapping the blossom and rubbing the petals gently against her daughter's soft cheek.

Lindsay kissed her and cuddled her daughter close. Happiness pervaded. She would take one day at a time, enjoy the strange turn of events and never forget that this was temporary. When Jonathan Balcomb died, she'd be like Cinderella and find the ball for her had ended.

Fingering the rose, she pricked her finger on a thorn. Sucking her fingertip, she grinned ruefully at Ellie. "That happens with roses, and with life, sometimes, honey. Even the most beautiful flowers can have thorns." Just as a sexy, dynamic man could have ulterior motives for wanting a marriage.

*   *   *

Lindsay fed and bathed Ellie for the night. The afternoon had passed quickly and pleasantly. She crossed the hall to her bedroom, warily peeking inside. No sign of Luke. With a sigh of relief, Lindsay grabbed some clothes and headed for a shower. Dressing again in her one nice dress, she brushed her curls until they shone. Dabbing a touch of perfume on her throat and wrists, she gathered her resolve for dinner. If tonight were a repeat of last night, she might ask for her meals in her room in the future. Such stress couldn't be good for digestion.

Taking the stairs slowly, she told herself she only had to get through dinner, a few hours in the living room and then she could go to bed.

To Luke's bed.

Her heart rate sped up. She wouldn't get out the blankets tonight. But would he wait until she was asleep again before joining her in that bed? The thought sparked interesting contradictions. On the one hand she would rather be asleep, convince herself he wasn't there. On the other hand, she was growing more and more intrigued with the man she'd married so hastily. Would he like to talk in the dark? Share the feelings he'd begun to reveal today in the study? She wished she knew more about him.

But exchanging thoughts like that brought an intimacy she wasn't sure she wanted. If she became too involved with Luke, she might not want to leave when the time came.

Pushing away the thought, she walked into the living room. Catherine sat on the sofa, just like the night before. Luke stood near the window, a glass in one hand.

"I hope I'm not late," Lindsay said.

"No. Marabel will announce dinner soon. Care for a drink?" Luke replied, his eyes roaming over her. She shivered, as if he had touched her. Her nerve endings hummed as awareness surfaced.

"Nothing, thanks." Except escape. Could she make it through the evening without making a fool of herself?

Dinner was not quite the ordeal of the first night. But Lindsay knew she would never be comfortable around Catherine. She was doubly relieved when dinner ended to hear Catherine invite Luke to her father's room.

"I stopped in right before dinner, and he said he'd like company tonight," Catherine said.

"I'll be right up. Would you care to come with us, Lindsay?"

She wanted to refuse. The last thing she wanted was to spend the evening with Catherine and Jonathan. But her sense of duty rose. She had agreed to this charade to convince a dying man his grandson was happy. He would doubt that if she never showed up.

"Very well."

Catherine frowned but said nothing as she led the way upstairs.

Lindsay wished she'd refused as soon as she sat in the chair that had been drawn near the bed.

"So, boy, holding out on me, huh?" Jonathan asked, his hoarse voice stronger than normal.

"How so, sir?" Luke asked, taking Lindsay's hand in his easily, lacing their fingers. He rested their linked hands on his hard thigh and met his grandfather's eyes.

Lindsay could hardly hear what was going on, mesmerized by Luke's touch, by his tender act. Of course she knew it was part of their pretense, but she didn't expect to feel so—so cherished when he claimed her in front of his family.

"When were you planning to tell me about the baby? That's about what, sir! I had to find out by accident. The nurse told me. I had to practically drag your wife in here with her."

"The baby?" Catherine turned shocked eyes to Luke. "You're saying Ellie is yours?" Outrage sparked in her eyes.

"Didn't tell you, either, huh? Dammit it, man, I know I overstepped the bounds with Jeannette Sullivan, but no need to hold a grudge forever. We've missed the baby's birth. It's past time you brought her home to her family."

"That child is not—" Catherine began.

"I'll speak for myself, Mother," Luke interrupted.

"Don't need anyone speaking to me," Jonathan roared. He took a deep breath and spoke again. "I asked the nurse to call my lawyers. I'll set up a trust for the baby."

"No," Lindsay said, even as she felt the jerk of surprise in Luke's hand.

"What? What's that? Why not? It's my money. I can do what I want with it."

"Do not leave any to Ellie," Lindsay said firmly. "Luke will provide for us. If you want to leave your money to someone, leave it to him."

"He'll get what I don't leave my daughter. Why not also leave my great-granddaughter a portion?"

"Because she is not—"Lindsay started.

"I said before I could speak for myself!" Luke interrupted. His grip tightened on her hand. "Jonathan, I appreciate the thought. I'm sure Lindsay will, too, once she calms down. But Ellie doesn't need another trust fund. I can provide for my own children."

Jonathan stared at his grandson for a long moment, then lay back.

"This is ridiculous. Ellie—" Catherine began.

"Mother!" Luke's warning was clear. The woman struggled for a moment, then subsided, glaring at Lindsay.

"A man has a right to leave his possessions however he wants," Jonathan said.

"You're right. If you want to line the pockets of your attorneys with more money to make yet another change when I can provide for Ellie without all that, go ahead," Luke said easily. Leaning back in his chair, he looked comfortable and relaxed. Lindsay knew appearances deceived. The grip on her hand conveyed his tension. She held her breath, wondering if Jonathan would back down.

Lindsay started to speak, but the squeeze of his hand

stopped her. She looked at him. Surely he wouldn't want his grandfather to leave anything to Ellie. She was not Luke's child.

He winked, then looked at his grandfather.

"Damn lawyers, never do anything without charging a small fortune. Especially when they think they've got a man over the barrel," Jonathan grumbled.

Lindsay hid a smile. Luke knew how to handle his grandfather. She should not have implied that Ellie was the great-granddaughter Jonathan thought she was. But if it made him happy, what was the harm? He wouldn't be around long enough for it to make a difference.

"She's a cute baby, don't you think?" Luke asked.

"Looks enough like you to be a female clone," Jonathan said, smiling, happiness shining from his eyes.

Lindsay smiled at that. Will and Luke looked nothing alike. While Ellie had dark hair, she resembled her father much more than Luke. Obviously Jonathan saw what he wanted to see.

"Bring her in tomorrow. I want to see her again. This makes you a pretty young grandmother." Jonathan turned his attention to Catherine. "I expect you'll want to shop all day long so you can dress her up in fancy dresses and show her off."

Catherine glanced at Luke, then smiled at her father. "I always thought little girls would be easier to deal with than little boys."

"Ha! Wait until the boys come around, then you'll see problems. Look at you—ran off with the first boy who came around. And left him a year later. You need to watch girls like a hawk."

Catherine stiffened at the reference to her marriage. Lindsay boiled over with curiosity. Catherine had left Luke's father after only a year of marriage? For some reason she'd thought the man had left. Thoughtfully, she studied her temporary mother-in-law. Why had that marriage failed? Was Luke close to his father? No, he'd mentioned

Jonathan was the only father he'd known. What had happened?

Marabel entered carrying a tray with slices of apple pie and a pot of fragrant coffee. She quickly served everyone, including a small wedge for Jonathan, and left.

When Luke mentioned that Lindsay had baked the pie, the old man looked at her. "So Luke's cook let you into the kitchen?"

"Lindsay is the mistress of this house," Luke said calmly. "She can go wherever she likes and do what she wants."

"I'm quite the guest now, Father," Catherine said. Glancing at Lindsay, she smiled politely, her eyes cold. "The pie is delicious. You are quite talented."

Lindsay thanked her and concentrated on eating as fast as politeness would allow. Then she would leave. Her stomach churned from the tension in the room and the deception they played on the ill man. She wished she had never agreed.

As soon as she could without giving rise to speculation, Lindsay bid the others good-night. She went to Ellie's room and checked on the baby. The small night-light cast a warm glow on the baby, who slept with a balled-up fist near her mouth. Lindsay touched her cheek lightly and drew the blanket to her chin. She was so precious. For a moment she remembered what Jonathan had said. She didn't think Ellie looked a thing like Luke. Was the old man's vision going? Or did he see what he wished to?

Lindsay put on her nightshirt and marched directly to the big bed. She refused to hesitate. She yanked back the covers, climbed in, switched off her bedside lamp and lay in the darkness. There!

She couldn't relax. There was too much to consider. Tomorrow she'd go to the bank and withdraw some of her savings to purchase a dress for the charity ball. While she was at it, she'd buy a couple more dresses to wear for dinner. Then she'd go home and collect her mail, maybe visit with her neighbor. She could be gone all day, let Ellie take her naps in her own crib. It would be better than confronting Catherine. The woman seemed furious at the deception with the baby. Lindsay sighed softly and turned on her side. Her intentions had been good, as had Luke's. Why had things gotten so complicated?

The dress was a dream. And a lot sexier than anything she'd ever owned. Midnight blue, it hugged her figure like a glove. There was a halter neck in front. The back gave way to criss-crossed straps that revealed her skin almost to her waist. Short enough to display her legs to best advantage, it moved like a second skin. Smiling, Lindsay studied herself in the three-way mirror. She didn't look as if she had a three-month-old daughter. Slim and fit, she looked as she had in her teens. If anything, carrying a fifteen-pound baby around most of the day had toned up her muscles and melted the weight off.

Studying herself in the long mirror, she decided she'd get her hair trimmed and splurge on some makeup. Luke would not have to worry about taking a waitress out in public.

Ellie scrunched up her face. Lindsay stopped and stared. "Is that a smile? Oh, honey!" She leaned over the pram and kissed the baby, excitement almost bursting. Some may say it was gas, but she knew that had been Ellie's first smile. She couldn't wait to tell Luke.

Hedley waited outside with the limo. When she was finished, he'd load the packages and safely put her and the baby in the car. Lindsay felt as Cinderella must have felt, odd, yet excited about the change in her life. She knew it wouldn't last. Midnight would come too soon. But until it did, Lindsay was going to enjoy herself. After she purchased the dress, they'd head for the Strand. She had some other dresses to buy.

She had not mentioned her plans to Luke or Catherine that morning. The last thing she wanted was to be coerced into shopping with Catherine. The dinner hour was more than enough time to spend with the woman. Lindsay wondered if she warmed up when Lindsay wasn't around. Catherine came across as cool and remote. What kind of mother had she made for Luke? Would she have really preferred a little girl? Curiosity rose again at the thought of Catherine's marriage. There was a great deal about the family Lindsay didn't know. And the longer she stayed with them, the more curious she became.

Did Luke like running the huge conglomerate? Did he really want to be responsible for so many employees? Had there been other professions he'd considered when growing up?

"All set?" The saleslady peered into the dressing room.

"What do you think?" Lindsay asked, nervous to have someone besides Ellie see her in the dress.

"Excellent! I think it was made for you. If you wear dark stockings and a diamond or two, it will finish the dress. Your husband may change his mind about going out and want to stay home," she teased.

Lindsay bit her lower lip and tried not to smile. She doubted she could compete with the beauties Luke was used to, but the compliment warmed her.

"I'll take the dress," she said happily.

Trying to placate and entertain a baby on a marathon shopping trip was no easy chore, Lindsay thought later that day. She was tired, but at least Ellie was asleep. They'd returned to their flat. It seemed small and a bit drab after the size and elegance of Luke's home. But it was her home, the one she'd return to when Jonathan Balcomb died.

Grateful for a few hours of respite, she put Ellie down for a nap in her own crib and waited only a few minutes before she heard the deep breathing denoting her daughter slept. Lindsay read her mail, paid a few bills, dropped one letter on the dining table to be answered later and swept the circulars into the trash. Quickly she dusted the flat, wiped down the counters in the kitchen. She wished Luke's maid, Tilly, was available to help. She knew the maid was a fast worker, and two sets of hands would make the work disappear that much more quickly. Still, the activity helped her remember this was her true life. The one she'd return to in a few weeks.

She had finished vacuuming her bedroom when the phone rang.

"Hello?"

"Lindsay?"

"Yes. Hi, Luke. Is something wrong?"

"You tell me. What are you doing there?"

"Here? Right now I'm vacuuming."

"What?"

"Vacuuming, you know, cleaning house. I didn't get a chance to clean everything up when Hedley—"

"Lindsay, if the flat needs cleaning, hire a service. You are planning to return home today, aren't you?"

Lindsay was tempted to tell him she was home, but she knew what he meant. Was there a note of uncertainty in his tone? Nonsense, the man had never been uncertain about anything in his life.

"I plan to have Hedley return me to your house after Ellie wakes up," she said primly. "Was there something you wanted before then?"

"No."

"How did you know I was here?" she asked.

"I called Hedley on the car phone when Marabel told me you'd gone out with him this morning."

"If you had been at breakfast when we came down, I would have told you myself," she snapped.

"Ah, missed me this morning?" he asked silkily.

Lindsay took a breath. She had missed him, had been disappointed he had left for work before she and Ellie had come downstairs. But she needn't reveal every facet of her feelings to the man. He already thought highly enough of himself, he didn't need her adoration.

Adoration? No—respect. Liking, maybe.

"Only because you weren't there to run interference with your mother. Of course I was lucky—your mother didn't come down for breakfast."

"Is she so impossible?" he asked. "If so, I'll send her home."

"No, don't do that. She wants to be near her father. And I'm sure she wants to be with you at this time, too."

"I doubt that. If so, it would be a first. Catherine thinks of herself foremost, all others a distant second," he said dryly.

"She is your mother."

"Much to her regret. I'll be home around four. Come home as soon as Ellie wakes up."

Lindsay stared at the phone as she replaced the receiver. What had Luke meant by that cryptic remark? She wished she understood the family better. She plugged in the vacuum in the living room. Her thoughts spun as she went through the motions of cleaning the room. Luke cared enough to call to make sure she was coming back.

What if he grew to care enough to want to be friends? Even after the need for their marriage ended? She'd learned a bit more about his business last night when he'd talked with Jonathan. She felt safe around him. And excited.

What a combination, safe and excited. And neither one was romantic. She wouldn't mind a bit of romance in her life. Will had been gone more than a year. Time to pick up the pieces and move on. But somehow she didn't see herself moving on with Luke. He was out of her league. Not that that fact stopped her fantasies.

Pausing in her work, she looked at the photo of Will on the shelf by the hall. His face smiled back at her. She eyed it thoughtfully. Will's eyes had been a light brown, his hair a shade or two darker. He seemed almost faded somehow when she compared him with Luke's black hair and black eyes. There was no future in comparing Luke with anyone.

Once his need for her was gone, she'd be on her own again.

Right now she needed to get her flat cleaned.

"I'll bring in the packages, madam," Hedley said as he held the back door of the limo open. Lindsay climbed out and reached to lift Ellie from the car.

"Thank you, Hedley, I would appreciate it. Come on, baby girl, we have time for a walk in the garden before dinner. Want to see the flowers again?"

Lindsay climbed the shallow steps and rang the bell. For an instant, she felt as if she were coming home.

She expected Marabel to open the door. Instead, Luke did.

"You need a key," he said, reaching out to lift Ellie from Lindsay's arms.

Before Lindsay could respond, Luke shifted the baby to one arm and reached out for Lindsay with the other. Threading his fingers in her hair, he held her head still for his kiss.

"Thought I heard the doorbell," Marabel said from behind Luke.

Lindsay backed up a step, flustered by his embrace. "We just got home."

"Don't we have a key for her?" Luke asked, stepping back, his dark eyes on Lindsay's mouth. Feeling flustered, she couldn't look away.

"I'm sure we have several keys available. I'll see she gets one before she goes out again," Marabel said.

"Good."

Hedley entered the hall, his arms loaded with packages and bags.

"I went shopping this morning," Lindsay explained, trying to ignore the fluttering in her chest. A kiss before the staff, part of the charade. That was all. She was an idiot for responding to it, for thinking it meant anything.

"So I see. Bought out a few stores while you were at it?"

"It almost seems so, doesn't it? I just got a few things."

"I'll take them up for you. I know you want to take the baby into the garden now. And as Mr. Balcomb is sleeping, Luke can join you," Marabel said as she began to climb the stairs. Hedley followed.

"Don't you have work to do or something?" Lindsay asked when they were alone. She couldn't help but notice how Luke's dark shirt molded his muscles, clearly showing movement when he shifted the baby. The snug, dark jeans made him seem even taller than he was, and he already towered over her.

"I'm free until Jonathan awakens."

The fluttering feeling grew as they walked together to the garden. Luke carried the baby to a grassy spot and laid her down on a small blanket. He reached for some of the flowers bordering the grass. He snapped off a half dozen and made a small bouquet, which he sprinkled beside her head. "But do not put these in your mouth, understand?"

"I'm sure she understands," Lindsay said dryly.

The little girl stared at him gravely, then looked at the flowers. Another smile started.

"Look, Luke, she's smiling. She did that today at the store. Oh, my, she's really smiling."

"Isn't she too young?"

"I don't think so. Just look at her, isn't she beautiful?"

"Beautiful."

Something about his tone caught Lindsay's attention, and she looked up to find his eyes on her.

"You are beautiful, Lindsay. So of course your daughter would be."

Heat stained her cheeks. "Thank you." It seemed so inadequate, to thank him for the compliment. Her heart pounded in her chest. Her breathing grew shallow. Swallowing hard, Lindsay stared back.

Luke looked away first. He watched Ellie for another minute, then leaned back, cradled his head in his stacked hands and closed his eyes.

"This feels good. I can't remember the last time I came out here just to sit. Maybe I've never done it before."

CHAPTER SIX

"IF I HAD a garden like this, I'd bring Ellie out every day," Lindsay said softly, her gaze focused on her daughter, her attention focused on Luke.

"You surprised me last night, Lindsay," Luke murmured.

"How?" she asked, leaning back on her hands, moving her eyes to study the different flowers, the clear blue sky. It was safer to her equilibrium than watching Luke.

"I thought you'd jump at the chance of having Jonathan set up a trust fund for Ellie."

"Are you crazy?" She swung her gaze around to him in stunned surprise. His eyes were open only a slit. If she didn't look closely, she would think he was almost asleep. "Ellie is no relation to Jonathan Balcomb. And I want nothing from him."

"Lindsay, Jonathan didn't neglect that truck, one of his employees did," Luke said softly.

"All to feed the important bottom line. I don't think profits are worth a man's life," she said hotly.

"Neither do I, nor would my grandfather. And I doubt the manager expected anything like that accident to happen. He was guilty of negligence, not murder."

Lindsay looked away. The result was the same for her and Ellie. They were alone. Will had been dead for more than a year. Sometimes she had trouble remembering him, remembering what his voice had sounded like, how his laugh had been so infectious, what a good friend he'd been.

"Lindsay?"

"I wouldn't take any money from your grandfather. I

97

wouldn't take it from you if I didn't need it so much. And I thought I was helping you out with the marriage.''

"You are. Any other woman would have milked the situation for a lot more."

"Well, I'm not another woman. And I wouldn't take your grandfather's money. I'd tell him the truth about Ellie first. I only pretended because he seemed so happy to think he had a great-granddaughter. Isn't that the reason for all this? To make his last days happy?"

"He's thrilled. He spoke about her after you left."

"I'm surprised your mother didn't set him straight."

"My mother is a rather selfish woman, but she loves her father. And she saw how excited he was. I don't think she wanted him to know the truth. She's willing to fall in with the story to keep his last days happy."

Lindsay nodded. "Why have this garden if you don't use it?" She wanted to change the subject.

"It's pretty. Sometimes I'll have a business dinner and it's a nice place to entertain."

"So where do you and your friends hang out?" she asked, taking the topic as far from the situation she was in as she could.

He smiled and closed his eyes. "Most of my friends are business acquaintances. I have to work hard to keep things expanding at Balcomb Enterprises."

"So what do you do to relax?"

"Lie in the sun and listen to a baby chatter."

She laughed softly. "Before this afternoon."

"Not much. I think I mostly work," he said slowly.

"No hobbies?" She plucked at the grass, tore a blade into confetti and let it drift from her fingers. It was peaceful in the garden. Ellie seemed to be dozing off, the colorful flowers like a halo around her head. The air was soft, still. It was quiet. Lindsay liked talking with Luke.

"No hobbies," he replied.

"Really, didn't you ever have any, even as a teenager? Besides surfing." She remembered he'd done that so well.

"No."

"If you could do anything you wanted, what would it be?" she persisted.

He opened one eye and looked at her. "Take you to bed."

"Oh." She didn't know what to say or where to look. Her eyes on Ellie, she fought the heat that scorched her cheeks and the longing that rose within her. She had never thought such a dynamic, virile man would truly want her. Swallowing hard, she sought for something to say, something to diffuse the tension that rose between them.

Luke smiled. "Is that all you have to say?"

"Well, actually, I don't quite know what to say."

"Forget it, I shouldn't have said it. Now you'll feel even more awkward about the bedroom situation," he murmured.

It certainly changed things. He'd said he wouldn't pounce, but he had never said he wasn't interested. Now that she knew he was, it colored her entire view of the situation. Especially when she was interested in return.

Lindsay scrambled to her feet, leaning over to reach for the baby. Luke sat up and looked at her.

"I'm not going to do anything you don't want, Lindsay. I'm direct in my way of dealing with people. I just wanted you to know that."

"It's time to take her inside. She's falling asleep, might as well put her in the crib."

Luke rose effortlessly and reached out to gather up the baby. She looked ridiculously small snuggled against his broad chest. For a moment a pang hit Lindsay. Ellie looked right in Luke's arms. Like she belonged.

Turning, she started toward the house, wondering how she'd gotten herself in such a mess. Thinking about Luke holding her daughter, about his surprising words, about her desire, which took hold and wouldn't let go, she thought she'd go crazy.

"It seems like it's two steps backward for every step

forward,'' Lindsay murmured. She wasn't sure where she stood, what to think. Or how to act. She dare not look at Luke, afraid of what he might see in her eyes. Desire, longing and uncertainty. If she wasn't sure what she wanted, how could she tell him?

But the knowledge that he found her desirable simmered in the back of her mind, bringing a warm glow. For the first time in a long time, Lindsay didn't feel like just Ellie's mother. She felt like someone special in her own right.

"Luke, Jonathan is awake now, if you want to see him." Catherine called from the French doors, watching them approach.

"I'll stop by a few minutes," Luke replied, "Right after we put Ellie to bed."

Lindsay looked at Catherine. The woman standing in the doorway seemed stiff and unbending. And very much alone. She looked at Luke. He didn't even glance at his mother, but his expression grew bleak. Suddenly Lindsay's heart went out to him. What had it been like growing up with Catherine for a mother?

"You don't need to spoil the child. She won't be here that long," Catherine said as she watched Luke hold the baby close.

"I guess our styles are a bit different," Lindsay said boldly, her head held high. "People are adults for a long time. I want my daughter to enjoy every minute of being a child. She can learn proper behavior before she grows up, but at this age she should be coddled and loved. She's just an infant. I never want her to think of herself as a burden or a problem, but to be happy and know she is loved. And that starts as an infant, with people holding her and loving her."

Luke met her eyes, his dark and mysterious. What was he thinking, she wondered. How would he raise a child, with a lot of love or by doing what was proper?

"Shall I tell my father you are coming?" Catherine asked.

"I'll be there soon," he replied.

Lindsay fought to keep her gaze away from Luke, though she was tempted by the sexy picture he presented. When had his hair become mussed? Lying on the grass? She longed to brush that errant strand off his forehead and then tangle her fingers in the rich thickness. Afraid to push too far, nonetheless she wished he'd look at her, maybe say something more about wanting to take her to bed.

Her heart pounded, and she smiled at Ellie, glad babies couldn't read minds.

"Lindsay?"

"Oh, she's waking up again. Maybe I'll give her a bath before dinner tonight. She likes baths." She was babbling but couldn't help it.

He smiled. "Need any help?"

"I thought you were going to see your grandfather."

"I'll let him know I'll be along after Ellie is settled. You can show me how to bathe a baby."

"If you want to." Lindsay was touched Luke offered to join them. How long before the novelty of the situation wore off? Before she left? Or would he still be attentive that day?

Bath time turned out to be fun. Lindsay laughed at Luke's expression when Ellie kicked in the water and splashed him. He played with the baby's rubber duck, bringing it close for the child to touch, then swimming it away. Ellie was enchanted with all the attention. This was how it should be, Lindsay thought as she watched the two of them. A family enjoying time together. For the first time she didn't think about Will, but about what it would be like if she and Luke planned to share a life together. They could have many afternoons like today. Quiet family time in the garden, at the children's bath—children? If they were planning to stay married, would he want a child? Or more than one? How would he feel about Ellie? It was fine to play one day with a baby, but to raise another man's child was a totally different matter.

Not that Luke had hinted he wanted to keep the marriage forever. Only until Jonathan died. Lindsay had best remember that.

"Mr. Winters." Nurse Spencer knocked on the open door and peered in. "Mr. Balcomb would like to see you and the baby. Shall I tell him you'll be in soon?"

"Yes. As soon as Ellie's dressed, I'll bring her in for a minute."

Lindsay looked at him, worried. "Should you?"

"Why not? He's happy to think she's his great-granddaughter, and if you can handle the deception, we'll keep it up a bit longer. She's a real sweetheart. He'll enjoy seeing her."

"At least she'll be clean. Can you manage?"

"Come with me if you like."

Lindsay smiled and shook her head. "Oh, no, *Daddy,* I think I'll let you solo on this one. If you want to build the story that she's yours, I don't have to be there every moment. Don't put her anywhere where she could fall."

Luke narrowed his eyes as he looked at her. "I run a multimillion-dollar company, I think I can manage one baby for fifteen minutes or so."

Catching her bottom lip between her teeth, Lindsay tried to stifle her grin. "Right. I have the utmost confidence in you."

"I'll admit I haven't been much around babies before, but I can manage this much," he said.

"When you two are finished visiting, I'll nurse her and then she'll be ready for bed." Lindsay watched him take her daughter out of the room with mixed feelings. For the second time she wondered what it would be like to make a life with Luke. When she'd been a girl she'd had such a crush on him. Gradually she'd forgotten all about him in the intervening years. But the awareness that crashed through her anytime he was near proved that the earlier crush hadn't completely disappeared. Given time, would it grow into something strong and lasting?

*   *   *

Luke pushed open the bathroom door and stepped into his bedroom, a damp towel wrapped around his waist. The quick shower had revived him. Now he had to dress for dinner.

"Oh." Lindsay walked in, hesitating by the door, her eyes wide as she stared at him. He could almost feel her gaze as it drifted across his chest, down his bare legs. For a moment he hoped the towel would stay in place, then put a hand on the knot to assure it. The last thing he needed now was to scare her away. Last night she'd shared the bed with no complaints. Maybe with patience and careful planning, they'd share more in that bed than just sleep.

"Come in, it's your room, too," he said, moving casually to the dresser. Maybe she wasn't as indifferent to him as she appeared. He could swear he saw definite interest in her eyes.

"I can come back."

"Don't you have to change for dinner?"

"Yes." Closing the hallway door behind her, she moved to the closet and pulled out a pretty pink dress. "I bought a few new dresses today to wear for dinner. And one that I think will suit the charity ball tomorrow."

Luke slipped into his briefs and pulled on his trousers, zipping them up before turning around. She carefully had her back toward him, examining the dress as if she'd never seen it before.

"I'm decent, if that's worrying you."

"No." She cleared her throat. "I mean, I've shared a bedroom with a man before."

"I haven't. Shared a room before, I mean," Luke said as he shrugged into a fresh shirt.

"Never?" She spun around at that. "I would have thought you—"

As the silence stretched out, Luke grew curious. "You thought I what?"

"Nothing. I guess in school or something."

"Something like what?"

"Nothing."

"Like an affair or two?"

"Well, you are over thirty, I'm sure you haven't been a monk all your life. And you were practically engaged four months ago."

"Did you sleep with your husband before you were married?" he asked.

"No. Not that it is any of your business."

"Maybe I want to make it my business." His voice was deliberately low, suggestive.

"You can't decide something like that. I decide what I want people to know about me."

"I'm your husband." He almost smiled. She looked so defensive, yet determined, standing by the open closet door, the pink dress clutched before her like a shield.

"Good grief, that's a lame excuse. It's a paper marriage."

"We could change that."

Luke watched, fascinated, as the color stained her cheeks. He wanted to cross the room, pull her into his arms and kiss her until neither could think straight. But he'd already shocked her once today. Patience, he told himself.

"I'll use the bathroom if you are finished in it." Lindsay clutched her dress tightly and quickly crossed the room to the open door. He heard the firm click as she shut it, followed a second later by the lock engaging. He shook his head. She was shy! Surprisingly so for a woman who had been married before.

More surprising was the growing urge to spend time with her. He had come home from work early and been disappointed that she wasn't waiting for him. The time in the garden had been special, different. He'd owned the house for a number of years, had quality furnishings, an attentive staff, yet it remained a place to sleep, eat, to entertain occasionally. Today, for the first time, he'd felt like he'd come home. He'd been relaxed and full of an odd sense of contentment, of completeness. Because of Lindsay and Ellie.

The feeling had extended to his visit with Jonathan. His grandfather had been delighted with Ellie. He'd insisted she be propped on the bed beside him for a while. Jonathan had looked better when they ended the visit. Could a child's presence bring that much happiness?

One as full of innocence and promise as Ellie probably could. She almost radiated light wherever she went. Her face had scrunched up into what her mother called a smile twice more. When he'd picked her up, he'd felt about ten feet tall. Glancing at his grandfather, he'd met his eyes.

"Nice feeling, isn't it?" the old man had asked perceptively. "I remember your mother when she was just that age. We spoiled her rotten, but she was so adorable it was impossible to resist."

It was hard for Luke to picture his mother as adorable. But she was Jonathan's only child and once had been a baby just like Ellie.

"It's a good thing to have a child, Luke. I hope you have more than one," Jonathan had said just before dozing off.

For the first time Luke wondered if he would ever have any children. His infatuation with Jeannette Sullivan had been ruthlessly cured. He was thirty-two years old and hadn't met another woman he'd wanted to spend his life with. If he didn't find someone soon, he'd be too old to be a father, too set in his ways.

Dinners were getting easier, or she was getting used to Catherine, Lindsay thought at the dining table that evening. She wore her new pink dress, one she'd fallen in love with. In the time spent in the garden, she'd acquired a bit of color from the sun. She was pleased with how she looked, and even Catherine's lukewarm comment about her dress didn't faze her.

The look in Luke's eyes when she'd joined them in the living room warmed her. With the echo of his words in the garden washing through her like an intoxicating wine, she was more than pleased with the result of her shopping venture. It was with great anticipation she wondered how he'd like her dress for tomorrow's charity event.

Of course, she still had tonight to get through. And the thought of sharing a bed with a man who had come out and blatantly said he wanted her set every nerve ending on alert. Could she lie there beneath the covers knowing he wanted her and not do something?

What if she snuggled up against him in her sleep? Would he push her away or take it as an invitation? Maybe she should consider the blankets on the floor again. Or find another room.

Coward, her conscience said. He'd promised he wouldn't pounce.

What if she pounced on him?

Shocked, she stared at her wineglass. She'd never thought of herself as the type. Even though she yearned for another kiss, longed to hear him say he cared for her, she knew she couldn't instigate anything. The attraction she felt for Luke was physical, pure and simple. She missed the companionship of a man, the feel of a male body in the night, the caresses and loving care. But Luke didn't love her. It wouldn't be the same as what she'd known before.

It might be even better. The insidious thought crept into her mind.

How disloyal to Will. She had liked making love to him. He had been the only man she'd ever slept with. Glancing at Luke, she acknowledged he probably had more experience. Would that make a difference?

"Can I give you something?" Luke asked when he caught her eye.

"No. I—sorry, I was just thinking of something." Lindsay felt like a fool and looked away, only to meet Catherine's scathing gaze.

"Are you going to that charity ball tomorrow night?" Lindsay asked, the thought suddenly occurring to her.

Maybe it wasn't a date between Luke and her. Maybe it was a long-standing commitment by the entire family.

"Yes. I didn't want to, but Father said he'd like to hear about the ball, so I'll stop by for a little while."

"Hedley can drive. That way if you wish to come home before we do, he can bring you back," Luke said casually.

"Did Lindsay get a new dress?" Catherine raised an eyebrow, as if disbelieving Lindsay could manage on her own.

Annoyed at Catherine's rudeness in ignoring her, Lindsay spoke up. "I did."

"Is it suitable?"

"I think I know how to dress for such an event."

"Maybe I'd better look at it later," Catherine said with condescending graciousness.

"Maybe pigs will fly," Lindsay muttered, glaring at the older woman. Tilting her chin, she spoke aloud. "When I put it on tomorrow night, if Luke doesn't think it's suitable, I'll stay home."

"I'm sure Mother was only offering her help," Luke said.

"I'm sure," Lindsay responded, holding the older woman's gaze. She didn't believe it for a minute. Catherine wanted to help no one but herself. And maybe her father.

Still seething from the attitude of her temporary mother-in-law, Lindsay excused herself early that evening to retire. For a moment her anger at Catherine pushed her concerns about sharing a bed to the back of her mind. They popped up when she opened the bedroom door. Marabel had turned back the covers invitingly.

"The last thing I need now is some sort of sexual attraction to drive me crazy," Lindsay muttered, kicking off her shoes. She reached to unzip her dress, some of the joy in her new clothes dimmed by Catherine's comments. As if she couldn't pick out her own clothes. Idly Lindsay wondered if they were quite proper. Was everything Catherine did quite proper? Hadn't she ever cut loose and had a bit of fun?

Dressed for bed, Lindsay pulled on a robe and crept across the hall to check on Ellie. The baby was sleeping angelically. Touching her warm cheeks, Lindsay felt the familiar welling of love threaten to choke her. She so cherished this precious gift.

"I wish your daddy could see you, baby girl," she whispered softly. Then the images of Luke playing with Ellie in the tub came. And the baby in his arms, his quick assistance in the garden, his taking her to see his grandfather. He would make a wonderful father. She wondered if he wanted children of his own.

When Lindsay awoke the next morning, something felt different. Slowly she opened her eyes and stared right into Luke's dark gaze.

"Good morning," he said. Propped up on his left arm, he had obviously just waked up. There was a sheet crease on his cheek, his hair was tousled and the covers had strayed to his waist. His chest was bare. Lindsay could feel the warmth of his body where she lay.

Her gaze danced across his chest, fascinated by the muscles, the light dusting of dark hair. Was it silky to the touch, or crisp and wiry? His nipples were brown, flat on the surface of his tanned skin. Feeling foolish, tempted, hot and bothered, Lindsay met his gaze.

"Good morning," she replied. Licking suddenly dry lips, she wanted to roll over, pull the covers over her head and hide until he left for work.

"Am I awake early or are you late?" she asked.

"I'm late. But I wanted to give you something. I had it yesterday and forgot."

He lay back, reached to the bedside table, picked up an object and rolled over until he was even closer to Lindsay. The mattress sagged beneath his weight, and she slid inches closer. Was he wearing anything beneath the sheet? Or did he sleep in the nude? Suddenly the need to know grew by leaps and bounds. It was all she could do to keep her hands to herself.

The soft cotton nightshirt she slept in didn't offer much barrier between them. Maybe she should get up.

Definitely she should get up, before she did something inexcusable, like reach out and run a fingertip across that chest, test the strength of his muscles, absorb the texture of his skin.

"What?" she asked, torn by the knowledge that her shirt, while it covered her, didn't exactly *conceal* her. It clung like a second skin and was short enough to reveal most of her legs. Getting out of bed probably wouldn't be such a wise move.

"This." He held up her wedding ring. Taking her left hand, he gently slid it on the fourth finger, then held her hand, looking at the ring, rubbing his thumb over it. It fit perfectly.

"With this ring, I thee wed," Luke murmured softly, then looked at her.

"With this ring, I thee wed," Lindsay repeated. It was the third time she had said the words. First with Will at the small church they'd chosen to be married in. Second with Luke at the registry office. And now. Would she ever say the words again?

For some reason they meant more today than four months ago when she and Luke had first said them. Of course she hadn't known him then. Not really. Just a fleeting memory of a teenage boy during her summers as a child.

Not that she knew much about him now. But she felt she did. And she felt connected to him somehow.

When he leaned over her to kiss her, Lindsay reached up to encircle his neck with her arms. It felt right and oh, so good.

His chest crushed her to the mattress, his hands threaded through her soft hair and held her. His lips were firm and warm and moved most persuasively until she was lost in the magic.

Ellie's distinctive cry through the monitor broke the spell his touch seemed to weave.

Luke pulled back, brushing his thumb across her damp lips, his dark eyes enigmatic. Staring into Lindsay's eyes, he dropped a light kiss on her lips and rolled over. "Sounds like Ellie's up for the day."

"Yes." Lindsay slid out of bed and snatched her robe. She wished she could brush her hair and wash her face before she faced him, but she needed to get to Ellie before the child really worked up a cry.

"Bring her down after you nurse her. I'll stay to have breakfast with you," Luke called as she hurried across the hall.

So much for getting time to think about things. His kiss had been perfect, gentle with a hint of passion held in check. Amazing what havoc it caused. Why had he repeated their wedding vows when placing the ring on her finger? She pushed open the door with her left hand, catching sight of the simple gold band that bound her legally to the man across the hall.

Did something else bind her to him? She swept across the room and lifted Ellie from the crib, afraid to examine her feelings too strongly. She didn't need any kind of attraction to Luke Winters. Certainly not one of any kind of permanent duration. Theirs was a temporary arrangement that would end very soon. If she had to keep reminding herself of that simple fact, she was already in big trouble.

CHAPTER SEVEN

LINDSAY had a moment of doubt the next evening when she donned the dress she'd bought for the ball. She spent Friday morning getting her hair trimmed and splurging on makeup. Her high-heeled shoes matched the dark blue of the dress, and the tinted nylons encasing her long legs made her feel quite elegant. The dress was perfect, unless she planned to keep a distance between herself and Luke. The impression given from the almost demure front would last only until people saw the back, or what little there was of it. It was pure allure. She felt delightfully sexy wearing it— she had never worn such a provocative dress before.

But then, she told herself as she tilted her chin, she had never had to compete with the women who would be present tonight or hold her own against Catherine Winters before. She was entering an entirely new realm and needed all the forces she could muster.

Lindsay hesitated, turning this way and that before the mirror. She had to go downstairs. Luke said he'd have the car out front at ten minutes to eight. The last thing she wanted to do was keep him waiting or give Catherine an opening for one of her snide comments. But now that the hour was imminent, she wasn't sure she could do it. It was one thing to have the saleswoman tell her how great the dress looked, something else to go down and face Luke. Swallowing hard, she took a deep breath. It was just a dress.

Nervous or not, if she was going, she had to go now.

Luke stood in the entry hall talking with his mother when Lindsay reached the top of the stairs. Taking another breath, she glided down the stairs, her eyes uncertain, her gaze locked on Luke. He glanced up when he saw her, his eyes

dark and unreadable as he watched her descent. He wore
the same tuxedo he'd worn to the café. She'd seen him in
suits, in a casual T-shirt and without a shirt. But he looked
wonderful in a tux and seemed even more distant and un-
attainable.

She hoped he would approve of her looks for this evening. She'd do nothing to embarrass him. Her heart began
beating faster as she stepped down another step and locked
gazes with Luke. The feelings that flooded her scared her.
She didn't want those feelings to grow. Their arrangement
was temporary only and would soon end. If she were to
avoid heartache, she had best guard her heart.

Her heart? Was she in danger of falling for Luke
Winters? Maybe she already had. No, she would not permit
that. Luke had been very clear that theirs was a temporary
alliance. She had the prenuptial papers to prove it.

Catherine turned and pursed her lips. Lindsay wanted to
caution the older woman about getting wrinkles if she
frowned all the time, but she knew Catherine would not
appreciate the comment.

Reaching the ground floor, Lindsay smiled tremulously.
"I hope I didn't keep you waiting."

"Hedley has been out front for five minutes," Catherine
snapped. Elegantly attired in a silver floor-length gown, her
hair swept up into an elaborate style, she was the epitome
of fashionable socialite. Diamonds glittered from her throat
and ears and flashed when she moved her hands.

"But then, he always arrives several minutes early,
doesn't he?" Luke said easily.

Lindsay smiled, grateful for his defense.

"Ellie asleep?" he asked as Lindsay crossed the foyer.

"Yes, she—"

"Good God, you can't wear that dress," Catherine cried
in horror when Lindsay passed her. "It's positively scan-
dalous!"

Lindsay turned in surprise and heard a soft sound behind

her. Turning to Luke, her eyes wide with question, she felt another pang of doubt. Was the dress unsuitable?

"Go upstairs and change immediately," Catherine ordered.

"Mother." Luke's voice was quiet, though the thread of steel that ran through it was unmistakable. "You are out of line. Lindsay is not a child to be ordered around. And even if she were, she is not your child. The dress is more than appropriate. You know we will see some outlandish creations at this event. There is nothing wrong with this dress."

Luke walked around Lindsay, studying her dress from every angle, then he smiled slowly, his eyes dark. "I think she looks lovely." He leaned close to her so she alone would hear him. "And sexy as hell!"

Lindsay beamed at him, heat engulfing her.

"There's virtually no back," Catherine stated.

"The back is cut low, but I wouldn't say there is no back," Luke countered. He frowned. "I should have bought you a necklace or something to go with it. Maybe diamonds for your ears."

Lindsay shook her head. "The dress is fine without anything else. And I'm not much for jewelry. I have my wedding ring." She held up her hand, and Luke took it, squeezing hard for a moment, his eyes gazing deep into hers. Was he remembering the vows he'd repeated just a short while before?

Catherine was furious, and Lindsay's heart dropped. The last thing she needed was more antagonism from the woman. But Luke liked her dress, and the heat she felt at his comment about being sexy warmed every inch of her. She wished just the two of them were going, that they could be spared Catherine's disapproval for one night.

"You will already create a flurry at the ball bringing her and introducing her as your wife. I hate to think of the speculation and gossip that will ensue after seeing her dressed like that," Catherine said haughtily.

"I think I can take it, Mother. As you mentioned, Hedley is waiting. After you?"

Luke sat between the women on the short drive. The tension in the limousine was thick and uncomfortable. Lindsay did her best to ignore it, looking out the window as Hedley swiftly drove across Harbor Bridge. The bright lights of Sydney sparkled as dusk fell. The sky was clear. Stars would be out before long, providing the perfect backdrop for the city.

The advantages of a limousine were clearly evident when they arrived at the Intercontinental Grand Hotel. The street was crowded with cars, cabs and other limos. Parking was impossible.

Spectators crowding the sidewalks watched as the elegant and trendy entered the hotel. The ballroom was huge. Sparkling chandeliers illuminated the scene. Colorful dresses, flashing jewelry and somber tuxedos filled the room. An orchestra played, and couples were already dancing in the large area in the center. To the left, tables and chairs offered places to sit. To the right, bars and tables laden with canapés lined the wall. Waiters circulated among the guests. People clustered in small groups, chatting or watching the dancers.

"I see the Taylors. I believe I'll join them," Catherine said.

"Hedley will return at eleven to pick you up," Luke said.

Catherine looked at him, "You won't be returning then?"

"We'll see how we enjoy ourselves before committing to a time. If not at eleven, Hedley can come back for us."

Catherine ignored Lindsay, saying that she would find Luke before she left and then turning to walk toward her friends.

Lindsay wanted to give a shout of thanksgiving but prudently kept quiet.

"She can be a bit of a trial," Luke said.

"She is your mother," she replied diplomatically.

"Would you care for a drink?"

"Maybe some wine."

When he placed his warm hand on the bare skin of her back, Lindsay's heartbeat doubled. Tingling awareness shot through her, and for a moment Lindsay thought she'd stumble. Her legs felt shaky, her back incredibly warm under Luke's touch. What would it be like to feel his hand on other parts of her body?

Lindsay waited near the bar while Luke waded through the crowd to obtain their drinks. She watched the couples dancing, fighting the urge to feast her eyes on Luke. Even so, she knew the moment he returned.

"How are you doing?" he asked, handing her a flute of wine.

"This is exciting! I never thought I'd come to something like this. Isn't that the prime minister over there?" She inclined her head in the direction of the man she recognized from newspaper photographs.

"Yes. Want to meet him?"

She swung around, her eyes wide. "You know him?"

Luke smiled faintly and nodded, his eyes watchful. "Through business."

Of course, the owner of a business as large as Balcomb's would know many influential people, including the prime minister.

"I don't think I need to meet him," she murmured, looking at the dance floor and sipping her wine. Its tangy coolness soothed her. Fascinated by the different dresses and hairstyles, she moved her gaze from woman to woman. Luke had been correct—there were many dresses more daring than hers. If no one went behind her, they might even consider her dress too demure for the evening. Her confidence soared. She had done all right. More than all right.

Sexy as hell, Luke had said. Warmed anew, Lindsay took another sip of the white wine.

"Care to dance?" he asked.

"Yes, thank you."

He chuckled softly. "Ever polite. Do you ever let loose and forget your proper manners?"

"Your mother doesn't find me very proper."

Luke's amusement vanished. "I don't care to talk about my mother, if you don't mind." He reached out and took her glass, placing it and his on a nearby table. Threading his fingers through hers, he drew her onto the dance floor. The orchestra had just begun a new melody, and he easily moved to join the dancers.

Lindsay knew she was dreaming a fairy-tale kind of dream. She was the princess and Luke the prince. They would dance with each other all night, magically finding their steps in perfect union, finding other aspects about themselves that meshed perfectly. She would be scintilating and he amused and entertained by her conversation. She'd entice him, enthrall him— Stumbling, Lindsay gave up her daydream and smiled apologetically.

"Sorry, I wasn't paying attention."

"You don't need to pay attention to dance," he said, drawing her even closer. She felt the strong muscles in his thighs brushing against hers, the sculpted muscles of his chest a hard rock against which she was pressed. His breath ruffled her curls, and his hands held her close without being tight. She could close her eyes and drift away.

"Lindsay?" he murmured in her ear.

"Mmm?" She did have her eyes closed. Smiling at the thought, she rested her head against his shoulder.

"Would you consider having an affair with me?" he asked.

She stumbled, then stopped in shock. Her eyelids flew open and she stared at him.

"What?" Had she heard him correctly? Had he just asked her to have an affair? Her heart raced. Had he guessed how she felt about him? Had he seen how attracted she was and thought to—what did he think?

He drew her close and continued dancing. "I can see I've startled you."

"Startled? Shocked me to death, more like. I can't believe you said that," she replied, her voice muffled against his shoulder.

"Why not? You know I'm attracted to you. I think you feel something. What would be more natural than we act on that mutual attraction?"

She swallowed. "I've never had an affair," she said blankly.

He smiled and brushed his fingertips up her spine. "I guessed as much. In fact I know your husband was the only man you've ever slept with."

She nodded, wondering if he could feel her racing heart, if he knew the confusion that reigned because of his comment. One part of her wanted to throw her arms around him, hold on tight and swear undying love. Another, more cautious part urged deliberation. She had to think this through. Maybe she should remind him that they were married, and married people didn't have affairs—at least with each other.

Only theirs wasn't a normal marriage. Would having an affair change that?

"What exactly were you thinking about?" she asked.

"You, mostly. Day and night. Do you have any idea how hard it is to get into bed at night and ignore you?"

They turned, moving across the dance floor in time with the music's tempo, going through the motions, yet Lindsay felt none of it, she was too stunned by their conversation. It was a miracle she didn't step all over his feet and tangle them up until they fell. How could Luke calmly discuss the situation and dance at the same time?

"Not exactly," she squeaked, dropping her gaze to his mouth. Remembering the kisses he'd given, she thought that not the best place to look. Her lips wanted to brush across his, rediscover the delight kissing him brought.

"Then think about it. You're a beautiful woman, sexy, loving. Who wouldn't want to take you to bed?"

"Is that all?" For some obscure reason, she was vaguely disappointed. Wasn't there more to her than just a body? "I mean, is that what an affair is, just going to bed together?"

"No, there's spending time together, doing things together, sharing things."

She cleared her throat, wished her breathing would slow before she hyperventilated or something. An affair. How exciting and scary. She wasn't the type to drive men mad with passion, yet here was an extremely masculine male wanting to start an affair with her. Such a thing would never happen again in the history of the world, of that she was sure.

Lindsay wanted to say yes, but she hesitated. She already had fallen for Luke. What would happen when their marriage and affair ended? She would be hurt beyond belief. Unless she could keep a close watch on her heart, make sure she never let herself dream about a happy-ever-after kind of relationship.

Would it be better to love and build memories to carry with her when she left or turn her back on this one chance?

"Lindsay?"

She looked into the dark eyes that so mesmerized her. Taking a deep breath, she nodded, afraid her voice would break if she tried to speak. Her aunt would roll in her grave if she knew what her niece was up to.

He tightened his hold, smiling at her, the promise of passion reflected in the desire he allowed her to see.

"Maybe we should leave now," he murmured. "We can send the car back for Mother."

"Oh, no," she said bravely. "I bought this dress especially for this ball and I want to get my money's worth! I haven't seen everyone yet, haven't met anyone, and I'm going to dance with you all night!"

"Change the rules just a bit and already I've created a

tyrant," he said dryly. "All right, we'll dance until the ball ends, but then, Cinderella, you go home with me, to bed with me."

The words thrilled her and scared her. Lindsay hoped she wasn't making the biggest mistake of her life. But for once she threw caution to the wind. They had weeks to build memories to last her a lifetime. She'd take the opportunity and worry about the hurt later.

As the evening progressed, Luke introduced her to people he knew when they came across them. Some they met standing near the bar, some exchanged names on the dance floor. Most of the people Lindsay met covered their curiosity. The notice of Luke's marriage had appeared in the Sydney papers at the time, but this was the first event to which he'd brought his wife.

"Is this what you do at these things?" Lindsay asked at one point when they were taking a break and nibbling on hors d'oeuvres.

"What do you mean? I talk to the people I know, meet new ones." He shrugged. They were near the buffet table, having just taken a few snacks from the lavish display.

"Did you ever bring your fiancée?"

He shook his head. "I was engaged a very short time before I found out how false it was."

"Like our marriage?"

"Lindsay, sometimes I think you don't believe our marriage is legal."

"Of course it is, Luke, you made sure of that to thwart your grandfather. It's legal, but it's not real." She took a dainty bite from a petite crab cake. She didn't want to spill anything on her pretty dress. Unsure if she would have a chance to wear it again, she knew she couldn't afford a second fancy dress if another occasion arose.

"After tonight it will be," he said heavily.

She looked at him mischievously. "Well, I do hope this won't change things too much. You've been a perfect husband so far."

He raised his eyebrow, recognizing the taunt as a copy of the words he'd once said. "How so?" Amusement lurked in his dark eyes.

"For the last four months you have not demanded dinner on the table at a certain hour. I don't have to do your laundry, and no one questions me on where I'm going or what I'm doing."

"That could change," he murmured, holding her gaze.

"Why would it? Surely people having an affair don't act like married couples."

"Lovers is the word you are avoiding."

Heat flamed in her cheeks. Before Lindsay could think of a reply, however, they were interrupted.

"Luke? It is you! How are you?" A tall, shapely woman stopped before him and smiled. Her auburn hair was long and fashioned in an intricate style for the evening. Her cat-green eyes never left his face. The green of her dress and gems caught and reflected the color of her eyes.

He straightened. "Jeannette, this is unexpected."

"For me, too, darling. I just got back to Sydney a couple of weeks ago. I planned to stop by and see you. We have a lot to talk about," she said, her fingers walking up the sleeve of his tux.

"I doubt we have anything to talk about." Luke stepped aside, dislodging her hand.

"Luke, I was a fool when you confronted me that night. I should have made it perfectly clear it was you all along that I wanted, not the money, not the prestige of Balcomb Enterprises." She rested her hand on his arm, and it was all Lindsay could do not to slap it away.

So this was Jeannette Sullivan, the woman who had conspired with Luke's mother and grandfather to snare the wealthy bachelor? No wonder he had thought he was in love with the woman—she was beautiful. Her skin was creamy and smooth, her coloring dramatic and bold. And her figure was to die for. The plunging neckline of her green gown showed off her attributes perfectly. Rather cynically, Lindsay suspected Jeannette had bought the dress with that in mind. What would proper Catherine say? she thought naughtily.

"What does that have to do with anything?" Luke asked politely. But Lindsay felt the distance. She wouldn't want him to talk to her in such a cold voice.

"Luke," Jeannette said, pouting prettily. "We meant a great deal to each other. We were in love. I foolishly let other things get in the way. I admit that now and apologize. Let's at least talk about it."

"I married someone else, maybe you'll remember," he said dryly.

Jeannette frowned, then her practiced smile slid firmly in place. "The little waitress?"

"Why does everyone harp on that particular job? I also was a student and worked in a bookstore. Yet whenever anyone talks about me, they remember I waited tables," Lindsay broke in, tired of being ignored. And just a bit concerned. Jeannette was stiff competition. Luke had asked for an affair not two hours ago. Would he change his mind now that he'd seen his former fiancée once more? Knew she was still interested?

Jeannette stared at Lindsay, her eyes narrowing as the smile faded from her face. "You're Luke's wife?"

"Yes. Lindsay Winters." It was the first time she'd said the name aloud. She had used Will's name until Luke moved her into his house. But it felt good to link herself with Luke. And they were linked—*married*. At least for the time being.

"Jeannette! I didn't know you were back in Sydney. You should have come to visit me," Catherine said as she and an elderly man stopped. Kissing cheeks, Catherine smiled at the younger woman. "When did you return?"

"I got back a couple of weeks ago. I did call, but you must have been out," Jeannette replied.

"I'm staying at Luke's. My father is quite ill, and I'm helping out until he recovers. You must come and visit."

Lindsay stifled a giggle. Catherine helping out? That was a funny line. But the rest of the scene was beginning to annoy her. She didn't need any reminder that she wasn't the bride of choice in this arrangement. And she certainly didn't want the lovely Jeannette invading Luke's home. She glanced at Luke. He watched Jeannette. Did he regret his hasty actions of marrying *the waitress?* Would he take Jeannette back now if he were free? Would they resume their relationship once his grandfather died and he could annul his hasty marriage?

Annul their marriage? Not if they embarked on an affair. Once the marriage was consummated, it would be divorce. Lindsay felt chilled. Somehow an annulment was one thing, but a divorce gave an entirely different slant to things. Did she want to be a divorcée? There was still time to back out. In fact, now that Jeannette was on the scene, maybe she should. Luke had made his point with his grandfather. He could safely marry his former fiancée as he had originally intended. Her heart dropped.

"See you later, Luke," Jeannette said, turning to walk away with Catherine, the two in close conversation.

Lindsay blinked. She'd missed the last of the conversation, lost in thought. When would Jeannette see him later? Was she planning to stop by the house to visit with Catherine? And would Catherine share her frustration about Luke's wife with Jeannette? Probably.

"Her timing was great," Lindsay blurted, eating the last of her crab cake. It was cold. She flicked a glance at the buffet table. Was there a new tray?

"What do you mean by that?" Luke took her empty plate and placed it on an nearby table. Taking her arm, he led her to the dance floor.

"I don't want to dance," Lindsay said, stopping abruptly.

"What do you want to do?"

"Go home, I guess. I miss Ellie."

"She's asleep. She sleeps all night long, how can you miss her?"

"I just do."

"Jeannette doesn't need to concern you," he said astutely.

"She's your fiancée, not mine," Lindsay snapped.

Luke smiled, but his eyes narrowed as he stared at her. Lindsay knew she was acting childishly, but she couldn't help it. Two hours ago they discussed embarking on an affair. Now the woman he'd once loved enough to ask to marry him—when not in a temper—was back.

"It's hard to have a fiancée when I'm married."

"Oh, Luke, have done. Our marriage has been false from day one. You married me in a temper just to get back at your grandfather. It served your purpose."

"In case you've forgotten, I want him to think I'm happily married, and that's why you are living in my home now. Earlier you agreed to an affair, so in another few hours we'll be sharing a bed in the traditional sense, not platonic sense."

"I expect Jonathan would be equally delighted to welcome Jeannette. He obviously approves of her. He picked her out for you!"

Luke leaned over until his face blocked most of the room. Anger shone from his eyes, radiated from his body. "He also thinks Ellie's my child. How happy is he going to be to discover she's not? Do we tell him we've been lying all along? That should make him happy—to find out in his last days that his grandson is a liar."

"You should have thought of that before embarking on this charade," she replied, wishing she could step back just a bit. He crowded her, almost scared her.

"No, you should have thought more about it before agreeing, before letting him think Ellie was mine. We continue. The man won't live out the next two months. The deal stands. All deals. If you want out at the end of that time, we can discuss it then. For now you are my wife and you'll remain my wife!''

His voice was low. No one nearby could hear him except Lindsay, who heard every word.

"All deals?" she said softly, her heart pounding again. Even after seeing Jeannette, he wanted an affair?

"All deals, especially the one you agreed to earlier this evening!''

"I don't think—''

"No going back, Lindsay.'' Luke cupped her chin in his palm and kissed her hard. "No going back," he repeated. Straightening, he pulled her into his arms and began dancing.

Lindsay held herself stiffly, conflicting emotions threatening to overwhelm her. She was jealous of Jeannette Sullivan, of her beauty, her self-assurance, her flawless rich background that didn't include working as a waitress. Even jealous of the warm feelings Catherine showed her. She'd been Luke's choice for wife. Only circumstances had altered their course. What had she been doing for the months since their engagement ended? Obviously she'd been away. Would they have met again before now had Luke not had to go to London? Would Luke have changed his mind and not asked Lindsay to move in? It would have been easier if he had.

Now he wanted all deals, including their affair. Slowly, the tantalizing thought invaded. Luke still wanted to make love with her. Lovers, he'd said. They would become lovers. Her heart skipped a beat. Tonight would be her second wedding night. And vastly different from her first.

As she moved to the music, Lindsay feared she was falling in love with her husband, but he had never hinted he might care for her. Not a moment ago he'd mentioned she could get out of the deal when Jonathan died, so there was no possibility of fooling herself into thinking this would last forever.

"Ready to go home?" Luke asked, seeing his mother approach.

"No. I don't want to go just yet." She had to think things through. Could she go through with what she'd agreed to? Everything had changed in her mind once she'd seen Jeannette Sullivan. The woman still wanted Luke. The question that dominated her thoughts, however, was what did Luke want?

Luke stopped by the edge of the dance floor and released Lindsay, clasping her hand in his as if to keep her anchored at his side.

"I'm ready to leave, Luke," Catherine said when she reached her son.

"We'll walk out with you and make sure Hedley is there." Without asking Lindsay to accompany them, he started walking. Her hand in his made sure she followed.

"It was wonderful to see Jeannette again. She's coming for tea tomorrow."

"Did you check with Lindsay to make sure that was all right?" Luke said.

"It's fine," Lindsay said quickly. She understood why Luke constantly reminded his mother that Lindsay was mistress of his house, but it always put her in the middle, and she hated it.

"Saturday is a good day, I thought. You'll be home and can catch up with Jeannette's news," Catherine said.

"I won't be home. I'm taking my wife and daughter out. So it's a good thing Jeannette will keep you company in the afternoon. We would invite you to accompany us, but I know you don't like the beach."

"But Jeannette expects to see you tomorrow," Catherine said, dismayed. "Luke, you must be there. You can take Lindsay and her baby out another time."

"I could, but choose not to. I mentioned before I won't be dictated to, Mother, haven't you learned that by now?"

Lindsay almost felt sorry for Catherine. She hoped Ellie didn't grow up to harbor the same feelings toward her mother that Luke showed his.

CHAPTER EIGHT

"FUNNY, I don't remember you inviting me and Ellie to go to the beach," Lindsay murmured as she stood beside Luke and watched the limousine pull away from the curb.

"It's a spur of the minute idea," Luke said dryly.

"As in you'd do anything to thwart your mother?"

He laughed and turned to her. "You are the only person I know who uses the word *thwart*."

Lindsay glared at him. "Don't try to change the subject. That's it, isn't it? You suddenly think up this idea of a day at the beach just so your mother will have to entertain your fiancée alone."

He gripped her arm, turned her around and headed for the ballroom. "First of all, Lindsay, my relationship with my mother or my ex-fiancée is none of your business. If Catherine wants to have Jeannette visit, she's perfectly capable of entertaining her. Secondly, if Jeannette thinks by crooking her finger I'll fall in line, she's in for a rude awakening."

Lindsay stared straight ahead, wishing he'd let her go. But when she tried to pull her arm free, his grip tightened.

"You must have cared for her, you proposed marriage."

"To the woman I thought she was, not who she turned out to be."

"Seems to me everything would have fallen into place."

He stopped her and swung her around gently, his expression impassive. "Would you care to be married for money?"

She shrugged, struggling with the sense of despair that threatened to flood her. "It's not much different from being married as revenge."

126

"I didn't marry you for revenge."

"Not against me, against your mother and grandfather."

Luke stared at her silently. Looking away in thought, he gradually released the hold on her arm. Lindsay fought the urge to rub the spot he'd held. He hadn't hurt her, in fact his warmth had her so confused she wasn't sure what they were discussing.

"Not revenge, exactly," he said at long last.

"What then, exactly?"

He glanced at her. Reaching up, he cupped her chin, his thumb brushing lightly across her lips. "As a means to *thwart* them," he said. "Come to the beach tomorrow. The weather promises to be beautiful, why not take advantage of it?" he asked.

"I didn't say going wasn't a good idea, just I didn't remember your mentioning it before." She wished he had wanted to take her and Ellie because he enjoyed their company, not as a slap in the face to his mother and Jeannette. But she'd take what she could get.

"An executive has to think fast. I have no intention of spending the afternoon with Jeannette Sullivan and my mother."

"Actually I can understand not wanting to spend time with your mother," Lindsay said as they sauntered into the ballroom. "Was she always so formal, so...distant?" she asked tactfully.

Luke steered her to a quiet corner and held a chair for her to sit. "Catherine's resented having me since before I was born," he said as he sat in the chair next to her. A waiter hurried over and took their order for drinks.

"Oh, no, Luke, that can't be. Your mother loves you, I know she does," Lindsay protested when they were alone again, or as alone as they would be in the crowded ballroom. True, Catherine wasn't very demonstrative. But how could any woman not love her own child?

He shrugged. "Maybe in her own way, but she has resented me from the beginning. She fell passionately in love with my father. But he wasn't from an old Sydney family. He was just an upstart whom my grandfather was convinced married her for the family money and position. Before long, I was expected and Jonathan ran my father off.''

"Ran him off?"

"Bought him off, whatever. He left Australia and never came back. My mother had the choice to go with him or return home. She chose the life she loved, not the man she professed to love. But she was stuck with me."

Lindsay reached out and caught his hand, squeezing in sympathy. "I'm sorry."

"It was over thirty years ago, not a recent event." Luke said dryly.

"It's pretty sad for both of you," she said gently.

"How do you figure that?"

"You didn't have a father while growing up, and she lost the man she loved. All because of money."

"Money counts a lot for many people," he remarked.

"I know that. But it can't buy happiness. That comes from within, from being happy with your life. Your mother finds fault in everything. It's a reflection of her own unhappiness."

"Well, she spends Jonathan's money like it's water to make up for it."

Lindsay shivered. "I would never want money to become more important than people. And I can't even imagine resenting Ellie."

"That is what sets you apart, Lindsay."

"I think you just have the wrong kind of friends. Most of the people I know are just like me. Did you ever try to find your father when you grew up?"

"No. I had Jonathan. I wouldn't begin to know where to look for my real father. He could be in England, New Zealand or the United States. Even dead, for all I know."

"I doubt he's dead. If he was close to your mother's age,

he'd be in his fifties. Did he even know you were expected?''

Luke looked at her in startled surprise. ''I never asked that question. I don't know.''

She shivered. ''Which would be worse—to have him know about you and ignore you, or be in ignorance himself all these years?''

''Hmm.'' Luke turned his hand over and clasped Lindsay's, rubbing his thumb gently against the back of her hand. ''Maybe I'll ask my mother one of these days. She's not very forthcoming about him.''

The waiter brought white wine for Lindsay and a whiskey for Luke. When he left, they fell silent, watching the dancers. The soft beat of the music soothed jangled nerves, and gradually Lindsay began to relax.

''Your skin is so soft,'' he said as his thumb traced patterns against the back of her hand.

''Are you changing the subject?'' she asked breathlessly.

''We've played out the subject of my parents. Now I'm trying to erase some of the stress of the evening. I still want you tonight, Lindsay!''

''Do you?'' she asked breathlessly.

''I thought I made that clear earlier. We reached an agreement.''

''That was before we saw Jeannette Sullivan.''

''She has nothing to do with us. The agreement stands.''

''I want you, too,'' Lindsay said, throwing caution to the wind.

''The best affairs start that way,'' he murmured, raising her wrist to kiss it gently.

Luke proved attentive all evening, dancing when Lindsay wanted, talking with men and women he knew, carefully introducing Lindsay to everyone. Once or twice she almost thought there was pride in his voice when he made it known that she was his wife. More wishful thinking, she admonished herself.

Lindsay was pleasantly tired by the time Hedley arrived

to pick them up. She sat back with a sigh against the soft seat in the limo. It had been a long day.

"Tired?" Luke said, sitting beside her.

"A bit." She almost held her breath. Would he kiss her now or wait until they reached home? Hold her hand? He'd touched her frequently during the evening, his hand like a hot brand against the bare skin of her back. His attention had flustered her. She didn't know whether he was truly interested in being with her or if it had been for show to the people who watched them tonight. Luke Winters was a well-known figure in Sydney's business scene, and many people had been curious about his wife.

Now they were alone. Lindsay took another breath, feeling as if the night closed in on her. Her nerves stretched so tightly she thought they might snap. In only a few minutes they would enter the bedroom they'd shared for almost a week. But instead of a pallet on the floor, instead of hugging the edge of the mattress, tonight she'd agreed to begin an affair.

Luke wanted her!

The thought warmed her at the same time it scared her half to death. She was not some glamorous socialite like Jeannette Sullivan. Her experience with the opposite sex had been very limited. What if Luke ended up disappointed after tonight? What if he didn't want to continue their affair?

She swallowed. Agreeing to such a thing had been preposterous. She had to stop it before things got out of hand.

"Luke?"

"Shh. We're almost home, Lindsay."

"But—"

His hand clasped hers. Resting their linked fingers on his hard thigh, he leaned closer in the cozy confines of the limo. "Shh. You're having second thoughts. Forget them. I'll take care of you."

Wishing he'd said some words of caring, she subsided and gazed through the window, seeing nothing but the tur-

moil raging in her mind. She was falling in love with Luke
Winters. Could she do anything more foolish? She wanted
to hug him close and make up for all the lack of love he'd
received from his mother, to make things right. Which was
silly. A more confident and secure individual she'd never
met. He may have lacked the love as a child that she showered on Ellie, but he had grown up beautifully. Maybe a
bit dictatorial, but who wouldn't be, fighting against
Jonathan's hold and his mother's indifference?

She turned her head until she could see him. Flashes of
light from passing automobiles let her see the beloved features, the strong chin, the taut cheeks, the lines near his
mouth that creased when he smiled. Which he did too in-
frequently. She wondered if having an affair would soften
those lines at all. He was a hard man, but she didn't fear
him. Instead, he excited her at a primal level that was quite
astonishing.

Feeling more alive than ever, Lindsay walked up the
stairs into the house and straight to their room, Luke beside
her every step.

He closed the door and leaned against it, crossing his
arms over his chest. "Are you all right?"

"Scared a bit," she said honestly, turning to face him.
Tossing her purse on a nearby chair, she stepped closer.
"I've never had an affair."

He smiled slowly, his eyes dark with desire. He reached
out and drew her to him, pushing her head gently to rest
against his shoulder. Lindsay felt electrified. Every cell in
her body tingled from the contact. She could scarcely
breathe, definitely couldn't think of anything but Luke.

When he threaded his fingers through her curls, she shivered.

"Cold?" he asked.

She shook her head—she was burning up.

"Let the games begin," he whispered, tilting her head
for his kiss.

*　　*　　*

The sun shone in the window by the time Lindsay awoke the next morning. She stretched, feeling happy and well loved. Slowly memories of the previous evening drifted into her mind. Smiling, she turned her head slightly. Luke lay beside her, on his stomach, head facing her, still asleep.

Taking a moment to study the man who had loved her so passionately during the night, Lindsay felt her heart quicken again. His dark tan contrasted sharply with the white sheets, making him look like a pirate. His hair was mussed, some falling across his brow. She longed to push it back, feel it again, thread her fingers through the thickness as she had over and over last night. But she didn't want to wake him.

He looked a bit younger, his features not so stern. But he was still rugged and masculine. And hers, at least for a while.

She swallowed, remembering how he'd been so gently loving last night, drawing a response from her she never knew she could give. It had been glorious! And he had not seemed to mind a bit about her lack of experience. He taught her things she didn't know, and together they reached heights she had never even dreamed about.

Wantonly, she wondered when he'd do it all again.

Suddenly Lindsay realized how late it must be. Had she forgotten the baby monitor? Turning, she saw it on the bedside table. She tested the on-off button. It appeared to be working, but she couldn't believe Ellie would sleep this late.

"Something wrong?" Luke's deep voice asked.

She looked at him and blushed, hoping frantically the color would be attributed to sleep. "I haven't heard Ellie. It's awfully late, she should have been awake by now."

"If she woke, Marabel would watch her."

"But hardly feed her."

"Maybe some juice. Didn't you mention you had started giving her apple juice?"

Lindsay nodded slowly, captivated by the man beside her.

His eyes crinkled at the edge as he smiled at her. She reached out to touch him, unable to resist. He caught her hand when she started to pull back and placed a hot, wet kiss in her palm. Moving her hand to his chest, he held it close to him.

"Good morning."

"Good morning," she said breathlessly, searching his eyes. Had last night been as special to him as to her? It was truly their wedding night. There would be no annulment. Pushing the thought of parting away, Lindsay smiled.

Luke pulled her across the distance that separated them until she was aligned against him. They had disrobed last night and never donned nightclothes. She felt his hot naked body along the length of hers, and the flames of passion rose.

"It's a good morning that's about to get even better," he said as he kissed her.

"I can't go out there," Lindsay said some time later. She had showered, dressed and now paced the bedroom while Luke pulled on jeans and a dark T-shirt. She sat on the edge of the bed, then jumped up as if she'd been burned and moved to a chair, glaring at the bed.

"Why not?" he asked cheerfully.

She'd noticed that. His mood was different. He radiated happiness. Well, maybe not that, but for Luke he sure seemed cheerful.

"Why not?" She looked at him and caught her breath. He looked wonderful. "Everyone will take one look at us and know what we've been doing."

"I hate to tell you this, sweetheart, but they don't have to look at us. It is almost noon. They already know what we've been doing."

"Oh, God." Lindsay closed her eyes and dropped her head on the chair cushion.

"It's no more than what they think we've been doing since you moved in," he said easily. "Or even before."

She sat up at that.

Luke nodded. "If they think Ellie's mine."

"Your mother knows she's not."

He shrugged. "Come on. I'm hungry. We'll get something to eat and head for the beach."

"We can't go now. I have to feed Ellie, then she'll have to take a nap," she protested. Maybe they could have a fight and she could stay in her room the rest of the day. The rest of her life?

"She can nap at the beach."

"It's important for children to follow routines," she said, grasping for straws. "We'll go another time."

"It's important that we get out of here before Jeannette arrives. Move it, Lindsay." Gone was the cheerful man of two seconds ago.

Sighing softly, Lindsay rose. Maybe the idea of a fight wasn't so sound. He would be a formidable adversary. Now that she'd shattered his mood, she wished she could take back the words.

They found Ellie in the kitchen being talked to by Rachel as she prepared salad for lunch.

"She must be starving," Lindsay said, hurrying to her daughter's side. "Hi there, baby girl." She nuzzled her cheek, taking in the clean baby scent of her child.

"She's an easy baby. We gave her some juice and she fell back asleep. She's getting fussy now, but has been good." Marabel rose from a chair nearby. Rachel turned from the stove and beamed at Ellie. "She's a doll to have around. But I'll bet she's ready for Mommy now."

"Your mother had a lunch tray with your grandfather. They will be finished soon. Do you want to join them?" Marabel asked Luke.

"No. We'll eat here as soon as Lindsay nurses Ellie. We're going to the beach when we finish eating." Luke drew out a chair and sat at the kitchen table. From the

glances Rachel and Marabel exchanged, Lindsay knew this
was not a normal occurrence. She picked up Ellie and escaped to the quiet of the nursery.

In too short a time, she was back. Luke sat at the table,
a plate before him. The place set next to him was hers.
Placing Ellie in the baby carrier on the table, Lindsay sat
at the place set for her.

Concentrating on the salad and rolls Rachel placed on
the table, Lindsay ate quietly. Too shy to look up, she gradually relaxed when she heard Rachel bustling around the
kitchen. Marabel leaned against the counter and talked quietly with Luke. She suggested it was time to replace the
drapery in the living room and wanted to know what Luke
planned to do about it.

"Talk to Lindsay, she's the boss here," he said, slath-
ering butter on a hot roll.

Lindsay looked up and glared at him.

"I like what's there now," she said. He knew this charade was temporary. What was he trying to do by implying
she really had a say in the house?

He met her eyes. "So do I, but if they are sun damaged,
we should replace them."

"Then replace with the same material."

Luke nodded.

"That was a special order, years ago, when you first
bought the house, Luke. It's not available anymore,"
Marabel said, looking between the two of them.

"Your turn." Luke said wickedly, amused by the angry
glint in Lindsay's eyes.

"I'll give it my utmost consideration," she said between
clenched teeth. Why was he doing this? The drapery could
wait another couple of months. She didn't think Jonathan
Balcomb would live much beyond that, not if Luke's as-
sessment was accurate.

"Finish eating, the beach is waiting," Luke announced
as if the other matter was resolved.

"Nice day for it," Rachel murmured. She stood at the

counter, glancing from time to time at the baby, smiling as if she enjoyed having the youngster there.

"We're not taking the limo, I hope." Lindsay said as she pushed away her plate. She couldn't eat any more.

"No, we'll take my car. More appropriate for a family outing, don't you think?"

A family outing? She nodded as the old dream resurfaced. She had thought she and Will and their baby would comprise their family. Now he was gone, and she was married to a man who constantly confused her. And drove her crazy. And made her feel sensations she'd never imagined.

Now they were in the midst of an affair and going out as a family. Ellie was still too young to do anything but eat and sleep. And now smile. While a good baby, she demanded a lot of attention and care. Would that annoy Luke?

"Get Ellie ready, I'll get Hedley to bring my car around to the front," Luke ordered when he finished eating.

Grateful for a few more minutes to herself, Lindsay lifted Ellie and headed for the stairs. She'd dress her in a sunsuit, then take a light blanket to keep the sun off the baby's tender skin.

Four hours later Lindsay leaned back in the front seat of Luke's BMW and closed her eyes. She was exhausted. The sunshine and fresh air would be enough to tire anyone, but combined with little sleep the night before, it was deadly. During the afternoon she'd needed to keep her defenses up when dealing with Luke. He constantly challenged her and teased her. She was hot, tried, windblown and a bit sunburned and had never had as much fun in her life!

"Tired?" Luke asked as he slipped behind the wheel and started the engine.

"Aren't you?" she asked, her eyes still closed.

"I think Ellie beat you to sleep," he murmured as he pulled out of the parking slot and headed the car for Sydney.

"I don't blame her. She had so much to see, she didn't sleep as long as I thought she would."

"Next time we'll bring a sitter," he said.

She wanted to open her eyes, but she was too tired. "If there is a next time," she murmured, almost too sleepy to respond.

"There will be a next time. But when we do this again, I'd like a little attention from my wife."

Lindsay opened her eyes at that. Was Luke jealous of the attention she paid the baby?

"Did you feel ignored?"

"No. But if I had wanted to go swimming by myself, I wouldn't have brought you."

"I had to watch her."

"I know. I'm not complaining. I'm still new at this, you know. I didn't think it through fully. One of us had to be with her, therefore we couldn't be together if we wanted to swim."

"We were when you carried her out," Lindsay reminded him.

"Yes." Luke smiled and reached for her hand. "I enjoyed today." He linked their fingers and held hers loosely against the wheel.

"I did, too." A warm glow splashed through her. It had been so much fun. And there were advantages to watching Ellie. While he'd gone swimming, Lindsay had been able to admire his body without his being aware of it. From the wide shoulders to his long muscular legs, she had reveled in the sight of him. Memories of long ago summers had surfaced. She remembered the lanky young Luke she'd had such a crush on. Remembered how she'd followed him and his friends, flirted, teased. Even then she had thought him special. But it didn't compare with the feelings she felt a woman.

She, too, wouldn't mind a baby-sitter the next tir

By the time they reached home, Lindsay had

Luke woke her and reached for Ellie, who slumbered even when lifted from the car seat.

"If you get her bag, I'll carry her inside," he said, waiting for Lindsay.

She slung the diaper bag over her shoulder and started up the front stairs. Her hair felt dry, her skin itchy from the salt water. Any makeup she'd put on that morning had long ago washed away. Hot and tired, she wanted a shower and change of clothes.

Luke opened the door and stood aside to let Lindsay enter first. She did so, and stopped dead. Catherine and Jeannette were coming from the living room, both looking cool and elegant. By contrast, Lindsay felt like something the cat dragged in. She wanted to turn and run, but Luke was right behind her, Ellie fast asleep against his shoulder.

Catherine's look of distaste was quickly masked. Lindsay wondered if Luke had even seen it. "There you are, Luke. Jeannette was just leaving. I'm glad you had a chance to see her before she left."

"Hello, Jeannette." His voice was cool, distant.

"A baby? Somehow, darling, that doesn't fit my image of you," Jeannette drawled in amusement.

"I'll take Ellie." Lindsay reached over and gently took her from Luke. Without another word, she turned and climbed the stairs.

"Stay a little longer, Jeannette," Catherine urged. "Luke, won't you join us for a quick drink?"

Lindsay paused at the top of the stairs and looked back long enough to see Luke nod his head.

"Sure, why not?" he said.

"_____ not?" she mimicked quietly as she carried _____ her room. "I'd much rather spend time with _____ orgeous and immaculate as you are, than _____ sunburned woman I married." Lindsay _____ s room, almost gritting her teeth. Damn! _____ h a wonderful afternoon together. Why couldn't Jeannette have been gone before they returned home?

Luke could have refused, a small voice whispered.

She lay the baby in the crib, found a warm washcloth, came back and gently wiped Ellie's face and hands. Tired as the baby was, she might not awaken for hours.

Lindsay put away the baby's clothes and headed for the bathroom, the monitor in hand. She'd take her shower and dress for dinner and ignore the fact Luke had preferred to stay with his lovely fiancée—*ex-fiancée*—rather than come upstairs with her.

Dressed, Lindsay paced her room. He still hadn't come upstairs. How long did it take to have a drink? Not that she cared what he did. She had no hold on him. Sighing softly, she acknowledged that was the problem. She was falling in love with a man who didn't care for her in the same way. Having an affair had been the limit he had proposed, nothing to do with making a life together, building a marriage. And she had nothing to complain about. She'd walked into it with both eyes wide open.

A gentle tap sounded at the door.

"Yes?" Lindsay opened it and saw Marabel.

"Mr. Balcomb would like you to sit with him for a while," Marabel said.

That was another thing. She didn't want to spend any more time with Luke's grandfather than necessary. She resented the man and all he stood for, and being with him weakened that resentment. Feeling sorry for his illness softened her heart. She almost liked the old man.

"How long before dinner?" Lindsay asked, stalling.

"Another hour or so. Luke's mother asked that it be put back a bit. That Miss Sullivan is still here. If she doesn't leave soon, they will have to invite her to dinner or go without," Marabel said sharply.

Lindsay nodded. Maybe that was Jeannette's plan. "Let me get the baby monitor, and I'll go."

"There you are, come in, come in," Jonathan called from his bed as Lindsay paused in the doorway.

Nurse Spencer smiled and beckoned her in. "I'll take a quick turn around the garden. Have Marabel come for me if you need me," she said pleasantly.

"Have a seat, girl, I can't be craning my neck watching you. Sit down," Jonathan ordered.

Lindsay pulled a chair closer to the bed and sat. Warily she watched the old man, noticing how frail he seemed.

"Been in the sun today, that's clear as can be," he said. For a moment he reminded her of Jack, the old cook at the café. Her resentment eased another notch. Given enough time, she might come to like the old man.

Nodding, she replied, "We went to Manly Beach." Self-consciously she wrinkled her red nose. The skin was tight and glowing. She should have used more sunscreen. At least she had lathered it on Ellie.

"You go sailing?" he asked sharply.

"No, just played in the surf. We had Ellie under an umbrella so she wouldn't get too much sun."

"Hmmph."

"Did you like to sail?" she asked brightly. Maybe he had been an avid sailor in his younger days. She'd never been, but thought it might be fun.

"No, didn't want anything to do with it," he growled.

"Oh."

He looked at her again, his eyes glowing with vitality so at odds with the wasted strength of his body. "Luke tell you about his father?"

"A bit," she admitted.

"The boy had some fool notion to sail when he was younger. I put a stop to that!"

Lindsay tilted her head, studying the old man. "Why?"

"Because of his father. Why do you think?"

"I don't know. All Luke told me was his father left before he was born."

"Paid him off, I did. Married Catherine for my money.

Well, I proved to him that he'd never get a dime unless he accepted my offer. He took it and left.''

"Too bad," she murmured.

"Eh? What's that?"

"I said that is too bad," she repeated clearly. "Luke missed having a father growing up."

The old man looked away. "Luke tell you that?"

"He didn't have to, it's obvious. He had no father, a mother who resents him and a grandfather who thought he could order him around like a lackey. Pretty rough childhood, if you ask me."

"Well, nobody did ask you, missy, so keep your opinions to yourself. Maybe I should offer you something to leave and see how fast you snap it up." His eyes came back, challenging her.

Lindsay smiled grimly and settled in her chair. She'd see just how far the old man would go. Then tell him all the money in Australia wouldn't be enough! He might think money could buy anything, but he'd find out soon enough that she couldn't be bought! "Offer away. I'll let you know when you're getting close."

"Close to what?" Luke said from the doorway.

CHAPTER NINE

LINDSAY turned in horror. While she didn't mind stringing Jonathan Balcomb along, the last thing she wanted was for Luke to think she could be bribed like Jeannette—or his father.

He leaned against the doorjamb, his face a deeper tan because of the day's outing. His crossed arms displayed taut muscles. His hair was wind-tossed, as hers had been, but on him it looked great. Lindsay swallowed hard, hoping the love that swelled within her wasn't blatantly obvious to the man.

"Nothing," she said hastily. "Hadn't you better change for dinner?"

Jonathan watched the two of them, his eyes canny.

"There's time." Luke looked at his grandfather.

"You might as well know I offered her money to leave you," the old man grumbled.

Luke's eyes moved to Lindsay, narrowed as he assessed the situation.

"And she just asked me to give my best offer."

"I did not." Lindsay turned to the man and glared at him. She wanted to see how far he would go but never had any intention of taking his money. He didn't know they already had plans to end the mock marriage. He thought he could buy her off like he had Luke's father.

"Jeannette would make you a more suitable wife than this waitress," Jonathan said, scoffing, his eyes alert.

"There is nothing wrong with waiting tables. I had to support myself because of you, you nasty old man." Lindsay rose to her feet and took a step closer to Jonathan's

142

bed. Luke moved so fast she didn't see him, his arm coming around her stomach and pulling her against his hard chest.

"That's enough, Lindsay," he said sharply. "Did you ask him to make an offer?"

Fuming, she glared at Jonathan. "I sure did. Just to see how far he'd go. Doesn't it bother you that your grandfather would try to wreck your marriage like he did your parents'?"

"What's that? I didn't wreck Catherine's marriage—she did," Jonathan wheezed, struggling to sit up.

"You did! If you had helped the couple instead of making her choose between money and her husband, they might have had a chance for a happy marriage. And Luke would have known his father. You stole his birthright from him. You are so greedy for money you don't care how many lives you ruin!"

"Lindsay, that's enough."

"I've not ruined any lives. Catherine chose a fool for a husband. I saw how the land lay and made him an offer if he'd leave. He took it. And I've regretted it every day of my life. I wanted him to spit in my face and tell me how much he loved my daughter. Instead, he took the money, and we never heard from him again. But in the long run, Catherine's better off. As Luke would be if you take the money and run."

"Why don't you let Luke decide that?" She spat the words out, her anger growing so fast she was furious. She couldn't forget Will. The ill man half sitting before her had been the person responsible for his death. Now he was trying to interfere again with his grandson's life.

"What decision did he have, missy, after being tricked into marriage because of a child?"

"Then I'll take my child and leave!"

"No, the child remains," Jonathan roared.

"Ha—shows how much you know, old man. Ellie is not—"

"Lindsay, shut up!" Luke lifted her and carried her from

the room. He let her go in the hall, and she almost stumbled. Reaching out, she touched the wall for balance.

He caught both her arms and shook her once. Lowering his head until his face was only inches from hers, he glared into her eyes, his voice low and deadly. "Dammit, the whole point of your being here was to show him how happy we are so he can die in peace. Instead you have stirred things up so badly, we may never get it straight!"

"I can't believe you're defending him. He was trying to bribe me to leave you. And he wanted to keep Ellie, depriving her of her mother! And you can still defend him?"

"He's my grandfather. He's half of all the family I have left," Luke said.

"And if not for him you might have a half dozen brothers and sisters, another set of grandparents and be married to the woman of your choice." Wrenching herself from his grasp, she half ran down the hall. "If he wants me gone, that's easily arranged."

"Lindsay, dammit, that's not—" The slamming of the nursery door cut off the last of his sentence.

Lindsay leaned against the door and looked guiltily at Ellie. The baby had slept through the loud noise, her dark lashes crescents against her rosy cheeks.

Adrenaline raced through Lindsay as she recalled every word Jonathan Balcomb had uttered. A despicable old man! She couldn't believe he had tried to get her to leave. Was it all because she had worked as a waitress, or was it one more attempt at manipulating his grandson's life?

How Luke could love an old man like that was beyond her. She ignored the fact she had started to like the old goat. He was as awful as she'd ever thought. But she held the key card. If he got obnoxious, she'd take Ellie and leave. There would be nothing he could do.

Gradually the turmoil settled. She pushed away from the door, crossed to the rocker and sat. Rocking slowly, she rested her head on the high back as she tried to figure out what she should do next. She refused to stay in the house.

If Luke wanted to play happy couples, maybe he should ask Jeannette to accommodate him. She could pack and get Hedley to drive her to her flat. Once Ellie was awake, she'd gather her things. Maybe she should pack her own clothes first.

Luke opened the door. He crossed the nursery silently and leaned over her, capturing her in the rocker by placing a hand on each wooden arm.

"You are not leaving," he said in a low voice.

She tilted her head. Could he read minds? "As soon as I can pack!"

"No." Stooping before her, he kept his hands on the wooden arms. "We made a deal, a couple of them, actually. I've lived up to my part, you will live up to your part."

"All deals are off. Or should I march into your grandfather's bedroom and accept whatever offer he makes?" She had calmed down for a few minutes. The anger built again.

"He is not making any offer. And you are not leaving."

Ellie made a soft snuffling noise and shifted in the crib.

"Come on, we'll wake her up if we stay here." Luke rose and held out a hand.

Lindsay ignored it. "She needs to wake up to eat or I'll be here during dinner."

"She can eat when she wakes, but let her do it in her own time. If it's when our supper is ready, we'll have Marabel hold it. Come on."

Lindsay debated whether to accede to his wishes or stand firm. He was right, she didn't want to wake the baby. Reluctantly, she put her hand in his and let him draw her from the chair. Holding her firmly, Luke led the way from the nursery.

"I can't believe you stood up for him. What if I took the bribe?" she asked as he led the way into their bedroom. Closing the door behind them, Luke finally released her.

"We both know you had no intention of taking his money. You were just baiting him." Luke pulled the T-shirt over his head and tossed it onto the floor. His hands went to the snap at his pants, and Lindsay crossed to sit down, wanting to stare at the body before her, too shy to do so. Her fingers tingled in remembrance of last night—how that sleek skin had felt beneath them. How the taut muscles had moved, contracting and expanding. How the very scent of the man had the ability to make her forget everything except the fact she was a woman. And that she loved him. She closed her eyes, almost groaning at the truth.

Luke's finger came beneath her chin, and he tilted her face to meet his. "He won't repeat the offer, I made sure of that." He lowered his face and kissed her gently. "I won't be long in the shower. Wait here, will you?" he asked, his voice husky.

She shrugged and nodded. Her gaze followed him as he walked into the bathroom. What would it be like to shower together?

Shocked at the trend of her thoughts, she swung her gaze away. Impatient, Lindsay rose and picked up his dirty clothes, tossing them in the basket in the large closet. Did all men expect others to pick up after them? Will had.

She couldn't compare Luke to Will. There was very little to compare, and she was afraid Luke would come out on top of every comparison she could find. Except for loving her. She never doubted Will's affection. Sometimes she wasn't even sure Luke liked her.

At least life with Will had been simpler. Neither had family living, so there was no mother-in-law who disapproved of her, no cantankerous grandfather who thought he had some right to manipulate people's lives. She sighed. When had life become so complicated?

Dinner was strained. Lindsay ate quietly, doing her best to ignore Luke and Catherine. Even if she lived there for six months, she knew she'd always wish she could eat elsewhere. Why did she have to put up with so much tension at a meal? A dinner at the end of a day should be a time to gather with people you loved, share what happened during time spent apart. Instead, at every meal she ached to be alone. There was no sharing at this table.

Catherine spent most of the meal talking about what Jeannette had said. How she had enjoyed visiting the United States. How glad she was to be home. How she'd missed everyone and how she knew now her trying to placate Luke's grandfather had backfired and ruined their love.

Twice Lindsay studied Catherine as she went on and on to Luke about his former fiancée. Was the woman deliberately trying to make Lindsay feel bad, or was she so insensitive she had no idea how she sounded? Lindsay decided Catherine was too smart to be so insensitive. She spoke deliberately.

Just before Marabel brought in dessert, the baby monitor conveyed the soft beginning of Ellie's cries.

"Excuse me." Lindsay rose and started for the hallway.

"Let Marabel get her. No sense in ruining your dinner," Catherine said carelessly.

Lindsay paused in the doorway and turned. "My daughter could never ruin my dinner. I'm delighted to have her and to spend time with her. She'll grow up all too fast and make her own way in the world. But I hope she will cherish the love we share and time we spent together as much as I shall." Lindsay ran lightly up the stairs and headed for the nursery and Ellie.

For the next two hours Lindsay stayed with Ellie. While Ellie nursed, Lindsay dreamed of the future, of the things she and her daughter could do. It would be only the two of them. Lindsay had loved twice now and didn't expect to find a third man. But she had happy memories of Will. Would her memories of her time with Luke be bittersweet?

Marabel peeped into the nursery. Lindsay had finished nursing and was patting Ellie's back as she held the baby against her shoulder. "I can watch the baby for you," she offered.

"Thank you, Marabel, but I want to spend time with her."

"After the day at the beach, I would think you'd want a break," Marabel said.

"No. You forget, I'm used to being with her all the time. Last night I really missed her. I hadn't been apart from her that long since she was born."

"She slept the entire time."

"I know, but still, it felt funny to be so far away."

Marabel laughed, nodding. "I have two boys. I know how a new mother feels. Call me if I can help."

When Ellie drifted off to sleep, Lindsay continued to hold her and rock. She loved these quiet times when Ellie was all hers. All too soon she'd grow into a toddler, then a little girl, wanting to explore and try new things. Asleep, she was soft and lovable and so sweet.

Even after it grew dark, Lindsay made no move to put the baby in the crib. She rocked slowly and thought about everything that had happened over the last several months. She had made a number of mistakes. The first had been to agree to marriage with Luke. The most serious had been to fall in love with him. He was too different, his background too far removed from hers. Long-ago summers at the beach didn't make up for the difference. They could never have a lasting affair.

Smiling, she could feel her body hum with desire. The affair they'd started would burn out. But what a blaze of glory until it did. How she would cope in the future, how she would deal with the loneliness and heartbreak was something she didn't want to contemplate now. She ought to plan for it, but she couldn't—not yet. Sufficient unto the day—

"Lindsay?" Luke said softly from the open door.

"What?" she whispered.

He stepped inside the nursery and looked at the mother and child. His eyes were dark. She couldn't read his expression.

"Is she asleep?"

"Yes."

"Put her to bed and come to ours," he ordered gently.

As if she were sleepwalking or drifting on a fine dream, Lindsay rose and tucked her baby in the crib. She flipped on the monitor, clipped the receiver to her waistband and turned to follow Luke. The bright light in the hallway caused her to squint in sudden discomfort. But the darkness of their bedroom soon surrounded them.

The door closed with a click. Luke pulled her into his arms. His mouth was hot against hers, urgent, demanding. She forgot about the future and the past. This was her present and she would cherish every moment. Flinging her arms around him, she matched his tempo. Her lips traced his, her tongue danced with his. Her body matched his along every inch.

Temporary lovers, temporary spouses, none of it mattered—only the fire Luke ignited then fanned into a blaze.

When the conflagration had died to warm embers, Lindsay snuggled against Luke's hard chest. Her hand rested on his arm. Her head was pillowed on his shoulder. Her breathing was still erratic, but slowing. She felt wonderful. Maybe things would work if they never left their bedroom.

Blushing at the thought, she closed her eyes, drifting toward sleep.

"Lindsay, I want your promise that you won't leave," Luke said, startling her into full consciousness. "I know you are furious with Jonathan, but running away isn't going to change anything. And I don't have the time or energy to be worrying about you taking off. I want your promise to stay."

"Aren't you afraid I'll try to get money from Jonathan to set me up in style?"

"Not for a minute. I know you better than that. If you were interested in money, you would have held out for more from me. Neither time when I offered it did you seem that concerned. No, mercenary is one thing you are not.''

Warmed by the trust he placed in her, Lindsay gave him her promise.

"No matter what happens," he added.

"No matter what happens." She hesitated, then lifted her head, trying to see him in the dark. "What will happen?"

"I don't know, but I believe in covering all bases."

"Hmm, sounds like a business move to me." She lay her head back.

"I am a businessman," he said.

"I know." Idly she traced the muscles on his arm, moving her hand to his chest, tangling her fingers in the hair that grew there. He was so fit. How did he keep toned working at an office all day? Suddenly she thought of something Jonathan had said.

"Luke?"

"Hmm?"

"Are you asleep?"

"Tired as hell, but not asleep yet, why?"

"I wanted to ask if you'd like to go sailing sometime." His body tensed. "Why?"

"You mentioned it a couple of days ago in the garden. And something your grandfather said tonight reminded me. Was your father a sailor?"

"He designed sailboats and built them."

"Have you ever been?"

"Only once. A business associate invited me on his boat a few years ago. It was quite an afternoon. I liked it."

"I bet it was exhilarating! Skimming across the water, moving silently with only the sound of the waves slapping on the hull and the snap of the sail in the wind."

"It was. The sun beat down, and once we had to tack to get to where he wanted to go. The spray as the boat hit some of the waves caused rainbows to dance in the wind. It was beautiful. And challenging."

"Man against the sea," she murmured.

His chuckle rocked her. "Hardly that. It was a perfect day. The challenge came from moving the boat where we wanted no matter the direction of the wind."

"But there would be times when it would be man against the sea. And I hope you'd always win. You should buy a boat."

"Oh, I should?"

"Yes. You should buy one right away and take me and Ellie sailing. Before fall comes. It would be a great family outing. And a perfect hobby for you. I can see you as a pirate or buccaneer."

Luke laughed.

"I'm serious," Lindsay protested, secretly enchanted with the effect of his laughter. She wished he would do it more often.

"A pirate?"

"Well, buccaneer, maybe. You know, a man who lives on the sea, wrests a living from it, and of course your natural cockiness would mandate a buccaneer, not a fisherman."

"Natural cockiness?" He rolled her over, then leaned across her as he held her pinned to the bed. "I am not cocky."

Tracing her fingertips across his lips, she smiled at him, wishing she could see more than his silhouette against the open window. The stars gave some light, but not enough. "Arrogant, maybe?" she teased. "Bossy?"

"Who's bossy? Didn't you just order me to buy a boat?"

"Sure, but that is to make you happy."

Luke fell silent. Lindsay could see him searching her face in the faint light from the stars.

"My life is fine the way it is," he said heavily.

"Do you love business so much? Seems to me all you do is go to work and visit your sick grandfather."

"These days my life isn't as routine as it was. Once Jonathan dies, things will change a bit."

"How, you'll spend more time at the office?"

"Or more time with my family."

She went still. Of course. Once Jonathan died, Luke would be free to start his family without any interference from the old man. Would he reconsider Jeannette? Would he let the past go and marry the woman he'd once asked to be his wife?

"No comeback to that?" he asked.

"No." Drained, Lindsay turned her head away. "I'm tired. I'd like to go to sleep now," she said.

"Jeannette is coming for dinner tomorrow," Luke said as he rolled on his back.

Lindsay felt chilled. She wished she had not made that promise to stay. Leaving seemed the only solution to avoid total heartbreak. Could she watch the man she loved interact with his fiancée? Maybe she could feign illness, remain in her room. She expected dinner would be a vastly different affair to Catherine, with an honored guest instead of an unwanted daughter-in-law.

The next morning Lindsay took Ellie out to the garden. The weather remained beautiful, and she wanted to take advantage of it. Luke promised to join them as soon as he checked in with a few things at the office. Lindsay gave him a knowing look, and he told her he didn't plan to work all day. She shrugged and left. She spread a blanket on the ground, gently placed the baby in the shade, than sank down beside her. It was so peaceful and pretty in the garden. The flowers were abundant—roses in all different hues, large banks of daisies, neat borders of deep purple petunias. The tall eucalyptus trees sheltered the area from wind, while the Morton Bay fig trees provided ample shade against the hot sun. Quite different from the beach.

When she heard footsteps on the pathway, Lindsay's heart soared. Luke had said he wouldn't take all day. Now he'd spend time with her.

Disappointment flared when Catherine stepped into view.

She hesitated on the grassy edge, then crossed to the bench near the blanket and sat.

Lindsay eyed her mother-in-law, wondering why she'd come. To give a lecture on child behavior or complain of inappropriate grass stains on Luke's wife?

"It's nice here today," Catherine said stiffly as she watched Lindsay pat Ellie's hand, took in the flowers scattered near the baby's head. "Do you think the baby notices the flowers?"

"I like to provide color stimulus for her."

"Seems a waste. I'm sure she's too young to notice."

"You don't like children," Lindsay said, her eyes on her daughter.

"I'm uncomfortable around them," Catherine admitted, also watching Ellie. "But then I've never been around them much. Maybe if I had, things would have been different." Her tone was almost pensive.

Lindsay glanced at her. "You had a baby yourself."

Catherine met her eyes, looked away. "And I had the best nurses and nannies money could buy. My father's money assured that."

Was there a hint of regret in her tone? Lindsay shook her head. She didn't believe it possible.

Catherine drew some snipping shears from her pocket and stared at them. "I came to cut some flowers for the dinner table tonight."

She hesitated, studying Ellie as she kicked her feet in the dappled sunlight.

"I don't remember Luke at that age. I remember him as a small boy, always chasing after something. We lived with my father at the time, and his backyard was huge. We had a swing for him, and later a fort." Catherine turned to look at Lindsay. "Whatever you think, Lindsay, I do love my son."

"You don't show it much," Lindsay replied.

Catherine shrugged. "I guess I'm not the demonstrative type."

"It's not just a physical thing, though I would think a hug now and then would go a long way, even if he is huge. It's more showing love by being interested in what he wants and then being supportive."

"I always support my son," Catherine said stiffly.

"Then why did he have to find a waitress to marry to thwart his family?" Lindsay asked. "I can understand Jonathan behaving the way he did. Look at what he did to you and your husband. Though from what he said last night he regrets it. But you should have stood by your son." Lindsay shook her head in sudden understanding. "Forget it. A woman who wouldn't stick by her husband wouldn't stand up for her son."

"That's a rather harsh judgment from someone who knows nothing about the situation," Catherine snapped.

"I know I couldn't be bribed to leave Luke," Lindsay replied. She turned to Ellie, wishing Catherine had never come into the garden. Wishing she would leave!

"It is hardly the same thing. You know Luke is successful. Thomas was young, poor. We were only in our twenties, and marriage to him showed me a totally different side of life. I didn't want to live poor all my life. You've been poor. Did you like it? I suspect a desire for escape had a lot to do with agreeing to Luke's outlandish suggestion of marriage. You went for the money, same as I."

"Not quite," Lindsay responded, guiltily aware that Catherine had a seed of truth in her statement. "I did agree for the money, but it was for my child. You expected a twenty-something man to have the material wealth of your father? Jonathan had to be in his fifties when you married. He'd built up his professional life until he had a comfortable or extravagant life-style. Luke is in his thirties. He also had time to build up a good career. And, lucky for him, he had help from his grandfather. What's to say your husband wouldn't have been as big a success as Luke by the time he was in his early thirties? For all you know he's twice as rich as your father by now."

Catherine stared at her, dumbstruck.

Lindsay glanced down the path toward the house. Where was Luke? Or Marabel? Or anyone who could interrupt this unwanted tête-à-tête with Catherine?

Reluctantly she turned to the bench. "It's really none of my business, Catherine. I'll be out of your life in a few weeks. If we can just tolerate each other until then, you'll never have to see me again."

"I wish I could be sure of that," Catherine said slowly. She watched the baby for another few minutes, her features softening. When Ellie grabbed a fistful of daisies, Catherine reached out to take them from the child before she could stuff them in her mouth.

"Want to hold her?" Lindsay asked.

Catherine hesitated, then nodded. Reaching out, she gently lifted the little girl into her arms, smiling at her. Moving to sit on the bench, she spoke softly to the child.

Lindsay watched, amazed at the change in Catherine's expression. For a moment it looked as if she actually cared about Ellie. Lindsay sat still, afraid any movement from her would shatter the spell. Catherine played with Ellie for almost ten minutes, then suddenly looked up, flustered.

"I have flowers to arrange for dinner. We have a guest coming." She handed Ellie to Lindsay. "Do try to wear something appropriate tonight."

"For Jeannette? Luke told me she was coming." Lindsay refused to meet Catherine's eyes. She had no inclination to give the woman another weapon to use against her. If she ever suspected how jealous Lindsay felt about Jeannette, Lindsay didn't doubt Catherine would use it, in her spite.

Watching the older woman cutting the blossoms, Lindsay wondered if Catherine would ever warm to her. She seemed to enjoy holding Ellie.

"Catherine." When the woman turned, Lindsay smiled at her. "Luke's buying a sailboat. He's always wanted to take up sailing. Maybe you'd like to join us on the bay one day.'' She could make the first overture. Someone had to make an effort if there was to be harmony in the house.

At the tightening of the older woman's lips, Lindsay stared.

''Luke has better things to do than buy a sailboat. What a ridiculous notion.'' She gathered the flowers and headed for the house.

Lindsay didn't think it was ridiculous. She'd heard his voice when speaking of his sailing experience. He wanted this. Maybe his mother wouldn't support him, but his wife would. And it was time the rest of his family realized it.

Lindsay said nothing of Catherine's visit to Luke when he joined them in the garden a half hour later. He teased Ellie by brushing daisy petals across her cheeks and let her try to bat them with her tiny hands. Twice he evoked a smile from her. Lindsay seemed more overjoyed by the smile than anything as she lay on the blanket and watched them lazily, feeling a deep contentment in the quiet afternoon. In a matter of weeks it would all end, but until then, she would let herself feel happy. Enjoy the moment and then leave without a backward look.

Lindsay peeked into the nursery to check on Ellie one more time. She knew she was delaying the inevitable, but she did not want to go downstairs. She'd heard the doorbell a few minutes ago, the murmur of voices that told her Jeannette had arrived. If she'd been smart, she would have been waiting in the living room when the unwanted guest arrived. Instead Lindsay had delayed dressing until after Luke had finished and gone downstairs. Now she would make an entrance after Jeannette had established herself in the midst of the Winters family.

On the other hand, Lindsay fervently hoped Luke had his emotions under control and that she wouldn't see any signs of affection for his fiancée. She didn't think she could handle it tonight, not after such a delightful afternoon.

If she delayed much longer, Luke would send Marabel

looking for her. That would be worse. Gathering her courage, Lindsay wished she could eat in her room. But that would never happen tonight. Pasting on a bright, artificial smile, she started down the stairs.

Entering the living room, Lindsay saw Luke wasn't present. Hesitating only a moment, she crossed to the sofa, wondering where he was.

"Good evening." Catherine eyed the dress Lindsay had chosen and then turned to Jeannette. "I believe you've met Lindsay."

"Yes. How are you?" Jeannette's smile looked as phony as Lindsay's felt. Reassured that she was not the only one having difficulties with this encounter, Lindsay replied and sat on one of the brocade-covered chairs. "Where's Luke?" she asked.

"He had a telephone call just before Jeannette arrived. He'll be along soon, I'm sure," Catherine replied.

For several moments silence reigned. Jeannette was frank in her appraisal of Luke's wife, and it took all Lindsay's effort not to squirm at the blatant perusal.

"Sorry I'm late," Luke said, breezing into the room.

Lindsay looked up and smiled, her heart tripping at the sight of him. He met her eyes and nodded. "You look pretty, sweetheart," he said easily.

Moving to Jeannette, he offered her a hand, but she rose quickly and reached up to kiss his cheek.

"I'm so glad you invited me for dinner, Luke." Her voice was low, throaty.

"It's always a pleasure to have you, Jeannette. You are as beautiful as ever."

CHAPTER TEN

LINDSAY looked at her hands, clenching them into fists. She didn't know whether to be more furious over the fact *Luke* had invited Jeannette or that he found her beautiful when he found Lindsay merely pretty. How petty. What did it matter? In a few weeks he would be free to seek a new bride. Or resume his relationship with Jeannette.

Lindsay suddenly knew she wished he would choose her. Her and Ellie. That he'd tell Jeannette she'd blown her chance and he'd found something better. He'd found a woman who loved him truly for himself, and not for the money at his disposal.

Yet he didn't know that. Lindsay tightened her lips. She certainly wouldn't tell him she loved him. She'd stick with the original arrangement.

Dinner turned out to be pleasantly enjoyable. For once Catherine concentrated on someone else, leaving Lindsay to listen with half an ear to the conversation that swirled around her and ignore what she didn't care to participate in. Jeannette made no bones about flirting with Luke. She sat to his right, with Catherine opposite. Lindsay sat opposite Luke, at the foot of the table. The three spoke of old friends and social events that Lindsay had no clue about. She was content to enjoy Rachel's cooking, watch Luke and wait for the evening to end.

Luke laughed at something Jeannette said, and Lindsay smiled. He almost stopped her heart, he was so good-looking. Masculine brows arched over his eyes, the dark orbs mysterious and intriguing. Sometimes they flashed with anger, sometimes danced in amusement. Twice now she'd seen them glow with contentment.

He was big and strong, yet held Ellie so gently, almost clumsily. And he seemed as fascinated by the infant as she was with him. He'd make a wonderful father, despite the role models he'd had. At least he'd know what to do differently.

"I was so distressed to learn of Jonathan's illness," Jeannette said.

Lindsay looked at her.

"It's been hard," Catherine replied. Her face fell for a moment. "I'm grateful he can be at home instead of hospital. My place wouldn't have been big enough for him and a nurse. Thank God Luke bought a place so large."

"I would so love to see him, if you think he's up to it. I know you are angry, Luke, for what Jonathan and I discussed, but truly, I thought of it only as a way to make an old man happy while still getting my heart's desire. The love of my life."

Lindsay wanted to throw something.

"I'm sure Jonathan would be happy to see you, Jeannette. We can check with the nurse. If he's feeling fit, we can take our coffee with him."

"The perfect solution. Jonathan will be part of the party, even from his bed." Jeannette beamed at Luke, pride and devotion shining from her eyes.

Lindsay frowned. She knew the woman needn't be so blatant. Luke would surely look her up again once his false marriage ended. And their affair.

For a moment pain struck. She drew a deep breath, trying to ease the sharp attack. They were having an affair, and that would end, too, and she'd be alone once again. But for the moment, Luke had pressed for an affair, and it was time he remembered it had been his idea.

"Luke, darling, why don't you tell Jeannette about our plans for a sailboat?" Lindsay asked, smiling brightly. Time she stopped being ignored.

Catherine drew in a quick breath. "Utter foolishness. I

hope that is some pipe dream of Lindsay's,'' she said, glaring down the table at her daughter-in-law.

Jeannette looked attentive, obviously uncertain which way to lean.

Luke met Lindsay's eyes and nodded, his face suddenly impassive. "I hadn't realized we'd progressed as far as actually planning for a sailboat."

"Well, why not? You've wanted to go sailing your whole life. Time to loosen up a bit from work and indulge yourself," she replied, holding his gaze. Her heart pounded, but he had backed her up—to a point.

"I didn't know you liked to sail," Jeannette said uncertainly.

"He doesn't. You don't need a sailboat," Catherine said sharply.

"Maybe no one needs one, but everyone needs to fill the dark places in their soul with waves of rainbows," Lindsay said, but her message was for Luke. If he wanted to sail, why not? "Besides, it's in his blood. His father was a sailor. Why wouldn't Luke want to follow in his footsteps?"

Jeannette looked at Lindsay, startled. "I didn't know his father was a sailor."

Lindsay smiled sweetly, savoring the moment. "As his wife, it's possible I know a bit more about Luke than you do," she said gently.

"I do not like the trend to this conversation," Catherine said regally.

"You're right, Catherine, it is a bit premature to discuss our boat when we haven't purchased it yet. Next weekend, maybe, Luke? Something that will work with a family, I think. We wouldn't want children falling out of it on the high seas."

"I'm sure we'll get a boat that contains all the safety features needed for a family," he replied easily, the amusement she sometimes saw moving into his eyes. "Mother, you'll have to come out with us and maybe give us some pointers."

"You sail?" Jeannette asked, turning her wide gaze to Catherine.

Catherine tightened her lips. "A few times, years ago. I'm not going out on any boat."

"It might bring up bad memories," Lindsay said sympathetically. She hadn't meant for the conversation to turn against Catherine, but she wanted some sign from Luke that he remembered her presence.

"I would love to," Jeannette said eagerly. "You may even want to give me a ride on some of your test voyages. I sailed a bit before I left Sydney and can't wait to get back in the harbor."

Lindsay pictured Jeannette bobbing in the water, having been knocked overboard from one of the luxury yachts that cruised Sydney Harbor. Somehow she didn't think that was what the woman had in mind.

"Don't mention sailing to Jonathan," Catherine said suddenly.

"Why not?" Jeannette asked.

"He can't take being upset right now. We are trying to keep things from him that could put him in a temper. He would not like hearing Luke plans to get a boat."

"I'm sure no one wants to upset him, Mother," Luke said, his eyes still on Lindsay. "When and if I get a boat, we'll decide what to tell him."

The subject turned, and Lindsay was cut out again. Whether deliberately or not, she didn't mind. She'd had her say and linked herself and Luke in everyone's mind. Whatever the future held, for the present, he was hers.

Luke ordered their dessert to be served in Jonathan's room. Marabel nodded in compliance and said she'd bring it up.

Catherine led the way to the stairs.

"Lindsay, wait a moment." Luke caught her arm and

stopped her, watching his mother and Jeannette continue up the steps. He looked hard at Lindsay.

"What was all that about?" he asked.

She smiled and shook her head. "I just wanted to be part of the conversation for a while."

"Why did I get the impression I was a bone two dogs were fighting over?" he asked silkily, his thumb stroking the soft skin of her arm.

"Why, Luke, darling, I haven't a clue." She opened her eyes wide and tried to look innocent as she smiled warmly into his face. The man was not an idiot. She was just surprised he called her on it.

"Affectionate all of a sudden, aren't you?"

Lindsay stepped closer, very aware that Jeannette had paused near the top of the stairs and stared down at them.

"I thought lovers were supposed to be affectionate." She almost dared him to kiss her.

And he complied, his mouth almost bruisingly hard. "I don't like games," he said, pulling back an inch.

"I thought this was all a game," she whispered. Her fingers threaded in the thick hair at the back of his head, and she pulled him that scant few inches, opening her mouth for his kiss, being honest in her feelings as she returned it. When he pulled away the second time, Jeannette had fled.

"You are playing with fire," Luke said, gently turning her toward the stairs. "And little girls who play with fire can get burned."

"Badly burned," she muttered.

"Right."

"Try being ignored the entire meal and see how you like it," she said, hoping to cover the turmoil that must show in her face.

"And what did you object to the most, Mother's rather obvious attempts to exclude you from the conversation, or my making no effort to include you?"

She darted a quick glance at him as they climbed the

steps. "Actually, I just wanted your guest to know I was there!"

"Jealous of Jeannette?" he murmured softly.

"Should I be?" she countered immediately.

"No. I will take care of Jeannette. You just need to remember you are my wife."

"And that we are having an affair."

"I haven't forgotten, have you?"

Lindsay shook her head. His very presence tantalized her, his scent awoke yearnings, his touch caused sensations to dance along her arm, his voice mesmerized her, his lips had fanned the flames he ignited. Suddenly she didn't want dessert, she wanted to close the two of them alone in their bedroom and not leave for a month.

"Behave yourself with Jonathan," Luke cautioned at the door.

"Maybe I should just skip dessert. That way you don't have to worry."

"No, I want you where I can see you."

"About time you two showed up," Jonathan's querulous voice greeted them when they stepped into his room.

"We're two steps behind Mother and Jeannette," Luke said easily, drawing a chair up beside the one Lindsay sat on. He smiled at his grandfather. "Nice to see a new face in the group of visitors, don't you think?" he asked.

"I'm glad to see Jeannette, though I'm surprised she came after the dreadful way you treated her. And you have some nerve to act as if nothing is wrong. Your fiancée and your wife. Quite a treat, eh?"

"Now, Jonathan, it's all in the past. Luke and I have agreed to be friends. And who knows, maybe some day we'll be very good friends," Jeannette said soothingly. "How are you feeling?"

"Worn out right now. That great-granddaughter of mine was here for a while. She's a cutie, but she makes me feel my age."

Lindsay felt surprise. She didn't know Ellie had visited

again. Marabel had been watching her. Had she brought her in? At her own instigation or to respond to the old man's request? Maybe he was softening. If her daughter helped, so be it.

"Your great-granddaughter," Jeannette said tonelessly.

Lindsay wondered if Catherine had told her the truth about Ellie. She knew Jeannette wouldn't be happy about keeping that secret if she knew it. But neither dare she endanger Jonathan's well-being. Curious, she wondered what Catherine would do.

"Nurse Spencer and I are planning to teach her to call me Grandpa," Jonathan said proudly.

"It's a little early," Lindsay said dryly.

"You never wanted me to call you that," Luke commented.

"Well, I was too young when you were born. I didn't want to be reminded of growing old. But, hell, boy, I am old. And if I live long enough for Ellie to call me Grandpa, I'll die a happy man."

Lindsay said nothing, her heart suddenly going out to the ill man. He infuriated her, and she wondered if she'd ever forgive him for the irreparable harm his company had done depriving her daughter of her father, but she felt sorry for him now. He was old, dying, and clinging to the thought of living long enough to hear her baby speak. If Ellie's presence could make his last days happy, she was glad. Maybe the lie hadn't been as horrendous as she'd thought.

Luke put his arm around her shoulders and drew her toward him slowly. "He's as happy as I've seen him in years," he whispered into her ear. "This makes it all worthwhile."

She nodded, the guilt over their deception easing a bit. It hurt no one and gave an old man some happy moments.

It was late by the time Jeannette left. Catherine went straight to bed. Lindsay walked around the ground floor with Luke as he checked the windows in the living room and study and turned off the lights.

"I think you should get a sailboat," she said.

"I know you do. You made that perfectly clear at dinner. Thank you for not bringing it up in front of Jonathan."

"He seemed to forget my tirade tonight."

"He was happy to see Jeannette. Her talk of the United States brought back some memories. He spent several years there when he was younger."

"So I heard."

They began to climb the stairs—just like an old married couple, Lindsay thought.

"Jeannette is beautiful, isn't she?" Lindsay blurted, unable to forget how Luke had complimented the woman that evening.

"She is a beautiful woman. Always immaculately dressed in the latest style, never a hair out of place."

"Mmm." He hadn't needed to expand on her comment.

He closed their bedroom door and gently drew Lindsay into his arms. His eyes were warm as they gazed at her in the light from the bedside table. "Jeannette reminds me a lot of my mother."

Lindsay raised her eyebrows. "Oh?"

"On the outside, the perfect lady. But on the inside, cold and self-centered."

Reaching up, Lindsay began to loosen his tie. She cherished the intimacy of being in his arms, of their affair.

"While you, on the other hand, are almost her opposite. Warm and generous and loving. I especially like the loving part." He lowered his head and kissed her, his hands already unfastening her dress.

In the week that followed, Lindsay permitted Ellie to spend as much time with Jonathan as Nurse Spencer felt appropriate. Sometimes she'd take the baby in and place her on Jonathan's bed, other times Marabel or Tilly or the nurse watched her. The old man delighted in the visits. He had Luke bring home new toys for Ellie and gave her one each day, never letting the fact she was too young bother him.

He watched her avidly, gently touching her hand or cheek. He laughed when she smiled and then repeated every instance to whoever would listen.

Between Lindsay and Jonathan there rose an armed truce. She tried very hard to offer no reason to rile him, and he seemed to suspect she would not allow the baby to visit if they were at odds. Sadly, Lindsay knew Jonathan was the closest thing to a grandpa Ellie would ever have, except for maybe Jack. She wouldn't even remember Jonathan after he died. She was far too young.

Afternoons, Lindsay took Ellie to the garden after her nap. Twice Catherine showed up. She cut flowers to place near the baby and smiled when Ellie rolled over for the first time. Picking her up, she wandered around the yard, as Lindsay had done, showing the baby the flowers and talking silly nonsense with her.

Lindsay was surprised the first time Catherine appeared but did her best to avoid any controversial topics, especially Luke's father or his sailing idea. She was intrigued with the growing interest Catherine displayed in Ellie. It revealed a side to the woman Lindsay would have sworn didn't exist. But the proof was there.

She and Catherine did not grow closer, but it was enough for Lindsay that the woman had taken to her daughter. Maybe it was a reaffirmation of life as her father grew steadily worse, or maybe just the universal pull of a baby.

Lindsay and Luke had already made an appointment for the coming weekend with a sales office specializing in small sailing crafts. Luke wanted something he could handle himself without a crew. Luke had given her a priceless gift when he married her—time with her new baby. She hoped he would buy a sailboat and realize a lifelong dream. If she caused that, she would consider the debt paid.

She was carrying Ellie across the entryway when Luke arrived home the next afternoon. He tossed a heavy briefcase on the nearby table and reached out with open arms to scoop Ellie up. Tossing her gently in the air, he smiled at her wide-eyed, solemn gaze. Then she scrunched her features into her familiar smile.

"You are going to make her sick one day," Lindsay said, laughing, intrigued with the way he'd changed in the few weeks they'd lived in his house. He no longer held Ellie as if he'd drop her. He seemed as comfortable around the baby as she did. And he even laughed more often—especially around Ellie.

Tucking the baby in one arm, Luke reached out for Lindsay with the other. It was a regular occurrence now. Each day the two of them met him at the door when he arrived home. He would hurry them upstairs and close the bedroom door behind them. Depositing Ellie gently on their wide bed, he'd then kiss Lindsay until she could scarcely stand on rubbery knees. While he changed clothes, she brought him up to date on what they had done during the day.

By the time dinner came each night, Lindsay had fallen more and more in love with the man who was temporarily sharing his life with her. She and her mother-in-law were no closer than before, but with the support of Luke behind her, she didn't mind as much. And Catherine did have other things on her mind with her father's illness.

Lindsay visited friends occasionally, stopped by the bookstore to keep in touch, ate at the café to visit Jack and ended up at her flat twice, once to give it a hasty dusting and once to get a few more things for Ellie. Each time she entered it, it seemed more and more alien. She had grown used to the beautiful house and garden in Kirribilli.

"Don't get too comfy in the lap of luxury," she admonished herself when closing the door after getting Ellie's rompers. "It's temporary."

Even knowing it would end someday didn't stop her from relishing every moment. She loved Luke and stored up a treasure trove of memories for future days. She teased him and argued with him and secretly exclaimed her love

over and over. He'd never know how much she cared. It
was enough that she knew.

Jonathan Balcomb died in the wee hours of Saturday morning. Nurse Spencer woke Luke with the news.

And everything changed.

Luke dressed immediately and went to see his grandfather. Then he broke the news to his mother. Catherine was
almost inconsolable, even though they had known his death
was imminent. She kept to her room, refusing to see anyone. Through the closed doors, Lindsay heard her crying.
She wished she could say something to ease her pain, but
knew Catherine would not want to see her.

Trying to keep out of the way, she took Ellie outside.
But she was aware of the activity in the house. Within
hours, the doctor had been and the ambulance had carried
Jonathan to the mortuary. The phone began to ring as the
word spread throughout Sydney. By afternoon, Luke had
installed one of his secretaries to answer the calls and deal
with the condolences as he instructed.

Close friends of the family arrived, coming and going all
afternoon. Lindsay heard the doorbell over and over as she
sat in Ellie's room while the baby slept. Luke had not asked
for her all day. She wanted to be with him, to help with
this, but he hadn't indicated that he wanted her. So she sat
alone and rocked and thought about the future.

Ellie rolled over and took a deep breath, settling down
into a deeper sleep. Lindsay rose and checked her, then left
the nursery. She'd look in on Catherine. She knew the older
woman didn't want her around, but she couldn't help be
concerned for her.

Knocking gently on the door, Lindsay waited. Nothing.
She eased it opened and stuck her head in. Catherine was
lying on her bed, a crumpled handkerchief in one hand,
staring listlessly out of her window.

"Catherine?" Lindsay said softly.

Slowly she turned her head. "What?"

"Can I get you something?"

She shook her head, her eyes filling with tears again.

Lindsay stepped into the room and closed the door. She crossed to the bathroom, found a clean cloth and dampened it with cool water. Carrying it to Catherine, she sat on the edge of the bed and sponged her forehead.

"This will help with your eyes. I know they're burning," Lindsay said practically, folding the cloth and handing it to Catherine. Luke's mother laid the cool cloth across her eyes.

"I knew he was dying. We all knew it, but I can't believe it," Catherine said sadly. For a moment she sounded like a little lost girl.

"I know. It's such a shock. I thought he was holding on fine," Lindsay replied, patting Catherine's hand. "Shall I get you something to eat? Maybe some soup?"

Catherine shook her head. "No. I'm not hungry."

"Water, then, or some hot tea?"

"Nothing."

Silence filled the room. Lindsay could hear the murmur of voices below. How many people had stopped by? How was Luke coping? If she couldn't be any help to Catherine, maybe she should go and see if Luke needed anything. Had he eaten lunch?

"My father really loved your daughter," Catherine said in a low voice. "I had forgotten how he played with Luke when he was a baby. I was an only child, and so was Luke. Maybe Jonathan would have liked lots of children."

"I think Ellie liked being with him. She smiled a lot. She'll miss him."

"She'll forget him by tomorrow. She's so little." Tears seeped beneath the cloth.

Knowing it was the truth, Lindsay refrained from saying anything.

A quick knock and the door opened. "Catherine?" Jeannette Sullivan entered. "Oh, Catherine, I'm so sorry. I came as soon as I heard." Jeannette hurried across the room. "What can I do? I can stay with you, help you find suitable clothes, answer cards, whatever you need."

Catherine sat up and caught the wet cloth in one hand. "Hello, Jeannette. I knew I could count on you." She glanced at Lindsay, but hesitated, as if unsure what she should say.

"I'll leave the two of you together, then," Lindsay said easily. She rose and left the room. She knew she was not the woman Catherine wanted with her at such a time. But she couldn't help wishing Jeannette had not been the one to stay.

She wandered downstairs and peered into the living room. There were at least eight people besides Luke. Most of the men were elderly, contemporaries of Jonathan, no doubt. The middle-aged couple near Luke could be friends of Catherine. Taking a breath, she entered and walked up to Luke, smiling at the couple.

Luke looked at her, his face drawn and tired. He had not changed from the dark jeans and shirt he'd donned so early that morning.

"Pamela, Roy, this is Lindsay. Lindsay, friends of my mother's."

"How do you do?" Lindsay smiled at the couple, then looked at Luke.

"Can I get you something?"

"No, everything is under control. Where's Ellie?"

"She's sleeping. We stayed in the garden this morning, and I'll keep her from underfoot when she wakes."

"This isn't a place for her," he said.

"I know." She bit her lip, uncertain what to do next.

"How is Catherine doing?" Pamela asked.

"She's quite distraught. Jeannette Sullivan is with her now."

"Good," Luke said, "Jeannette will help her through this. I'll tell Mother when she comes down that you two stopped by. I appreciate it."

"Anything we can do, let us know. We'll call Catherine tomorrow and speak to her ourselves."

"Fine."

"Luke." Another man paused at Luke's elbow. "Can't believe it."

"I know." Luke's voice was patient, though he must have heard the refrain a dozen times. He glanced at Lindsay. "You don't have to hang around. I don't know how long people will be coming."

"All right." She said goodbye to Pamela and Roy and left the room, feeling awkward and unwanted. She didn't know the people calling, didn't know what to say at a time like this. Unable to be of any help to Luke made her irritable. She wanted to do something to ease this time for him, help him through it, not be shunted aside like unwanted baggage.

Which could be exactly how he saw her. Wasn't their agreement until Jonathan died? All deals were off now. She had fulfilled her purpose. The reason for their marriage ended. Luke no longer needed her.

Luke didn't come to bed that night. Lindsay lay awake long after she'd turned off the light, waiting for him to come. Finally she gave up. She didn't know where he slept, but it wasn't with her. Sunday, she took Ellie and had Hedley drive her to the flat. She called some friends and chatted, trying to ease into her normal routine. Arranging to meet a couple for lunch at the end of the week, she felt better. At least somewhere people liked her for herself.

After the baby's nap, they returned to Luke's house. Today the crowd was different, and Catherine sat in the living room. Jeannette sat beside her, her solicitation obvious. Lindsay felt almost invisible as she and Ellie walked up the stairs. She wondered if anyone had even noticed they were gone that day.

The funeral was held Monday. Lindsay asked Tilly to watch the baby and put on the dark suit she'd brought from home. There were dark circles beneath her eyes, evidence of her lack of sleep. Luke had not shared their bed since Friday night.

As she descended the stairs, she noticed how quiet the house seemed. Of course there were no visitors present. After the funeral, several dozen people had been invited to the house, but right now it was silent. Lindsay looked in the living room. Luke stared out the window. He was dressed in a dark suit. When he turned, she saw the pristine white shirt and somber tie. He looked exhausted.

"Hi," she said softly.

"Hi."

"I'm sorry it's been so rough," she said.

"Yeah. I thought we were prepared. I guess one never is."

She shook her head.

"You don't have to go today if you'd prefer not," he said.

"Would you rather I stayed away?" Maybe he didn't want her even to give a token appearance. Maybe he wanted to end the marriage as fast as possible, now that their reason for being married was gone.

"No. I just thought you might be going out of duty. And I wanted you to know you don't have to."

"I'm going to be with you," she said.

Just then voices drifted in from upstairs.

Catherine and Jeannette entered. Catherine had regained some of her coloring, though the stark black dress did nothing to enhance her looks. It was chic and expensive and looked quite elegant. The diamonds at her throat and fingers may have been subdued to her, but Lindsay thought they were a bit too much for a funeral.

Jeannette looked stunning. Her black suit jacket plunged in front, the fitted skirt was exactly that, fitted, and far too short in Lindsay's opinion. But she didn't think of a funeral as a fashion statement. These women obviously did. One disparaging glance from Catherine convinced Lindsay she was on the road to recovery.

Lindsay took a deep breath. It would be another long day.

The guests who returned after the funeral filled the ground floor and spilled out into the garden. The weather was balmy, the sun shone and the flowers looked perfect. Lindsay took a cup of punch and wandered around, again feeling almost invisible. Luke and Jeannette and Catherine knew everyone. With Jeannette almost Catherine's shadow, she was included in all the family conversations. Never once did Luke search for her, Lindsay thought. And why would he?

She found a deserted bench and sat down, wishing Ellie was with her. Tilly watched her in the nursery, and Ellie was probably sleeping through all the turmoil.

"I'll miss Jonathan." Jeannette approached across the grass and sat beside Lindsay. "He was a bossy old man, but lovable in his own way. I know Luke will miss him, too."

"Of course, he was his grandfather."

"Mm. I understand you and Luke pretended to be happy for Jonathan's sake. I'd like to thank you for that."

"Thank me?" Lindsay looked at her, perplexed.

"Yes. For making an ill man's last days happy. I know it would have distressed him to have Luke in the midst of a divorce when he was dying."

"Oh."

Jeannette looked all around at the garden, waving casually to an acquaintance across the way. "I've always loved this garden. I won't change a thing when—I mean—oh, dear. Have I put my foot in it?"

"You've discussed marriage with Luke?" Lindsay asked, hoping she could mask the pain that was beginning to spread through her. Her heart kept beating, her lungs kept breathing, but something died inside.

"Yes." Jeannette looked at her with sympathy. "I

thought you knew. I'm sorry, I wouldn't have said anything
if I hadn't thought you knew.''

"I knew.'' Lindsay rose and walked away. She refused
to sit with Jeannette another moment. Luke had ignored her
for days, not shared his room nor his thoughts. But he'd
found the time to discuss marriage with Jeannette. When
was he planning to discuss their divorce?

She moved through the crowd as if she were in a dream.
Reaching the nursery, she thanked Tilly for watching Ellie
and waited until the woman left before hurrying to pack
Ellie's things.

"Dream time is over, baby girl. Time we go walkabout.''

CHAPTER ELEVEN

LINDSAY cried herself to sleep Monday night. She missed Luke, missed the warmth of him in her bed, missed the touches and caresses and the man. But she knew it was time to move on with her life. She just wished he'd been the one to tell her, not Jeannette.

Tuesday she unpacked and visited her neighbor. She took Ellie for a walk in the park, watching her stare at the eucalyptus leaves dancing in the wind and remembering Luke's garden. There were no flowers here for a baby to play with. But the grass was green and the sky blue and the air balmy and warm.

Instead of lifting her spirits, it made her feel worse.

Her heart actually ached. She knew she'd get over Luke—maybe by the time she was a hundred. But the day seemed empty and barren.

Wednesday Lindsay left Ellie with Mrs. Heinemyer and took the bus to the bookstore. She asked the manager if there were any openings, and when he offered her her old job, she accepted. She hated to be away from Ellie for part of the day, but it was time to plan for the future. The savings she'd built up over the last couple of months wouldn't last forever. She wanted to keep them for an emergency. At least she thought she could manage with the one job. She hoped she didn't have to return to work at the café, as well. Jack would scold her if she even suggested the idea. But he still thought Luke the best choice for her. As she did herself. Too bad Luke didn't think so.

As to the trust fund Luke had promised, she didn't want it. She'd done her part for the marriage, gone beyond the original intent and provided his grandfather with the impression his grandson was happily married. It was fair exchange for the joy of spending Ellie's first months with her without money worries.

Luke had no obligation to provide for them in the future. Once the divorce was final, all ties would be severed.

Lindsay picked Ellie up after her nap, staying only a moment to chat with Alice Heinemyer. She wanted to get home.

"Did you have a good time?" she asked as they walked down the stairs to their flat. Mrs. Heinemyer had agreed to watch Ellie while Lindsay worked. It was a good arrangement. Mrs. Heinemyer had known the baby since her birth, and Lindsay knew the older woman would be a good person to watch Ellie. Her care would enable Lindsay to manage on the wages from the bookstore.

"You'll get to see her lots from now on." Lindsay's voice almost broke as the realization that she would be parted from her precious baby for hours every day took hold.

Reaching her floor, she stopped suddenly. Luke leaned against the wall by the door.

"Where the hell have you been?" he growled.

"What are you doing here?" she asked, shocked to see him. Shocked at his appearance. His suit was pressed and immaculate as always, but the lines around his eyes, the ones bracketing his mouth, hadn't been there a week ago. He looked tired to death.

"I realize that Jonathan was not your favorite man. I appreciate your attending his funeral. But you could have waited a day or two before lighting out. I know our agreement was to pretend to be married until he died, but did you have to leave so soon?"

Ellie's head swiveled at the sound of Luke's voice. She smiled, reached out toward the man.

Lindsay wanted to tell him she didn't have to leave at all, if he had only given the slightest hint he'd like her to stay. But instead, he'd talked of marriage to Jeannette. She wanted a lot of things, but a confrontation with Luke this afternoon wasn't one of them.

She frowned at Ellie when Luke lifted her from the baby carrier and held her in his arms, patting her back. The baby was pleased as punch to see him. She reached out a steady hand and batted his tie.

"There was no reason to drag it out," Lindsay said. Fumbling for her keys, she resented his taking them from her hand and opening the door so easily, especially with Ellie in one arm. It would be impossible to close the door in his face. Had he planned that? She wouldn't put it past him. If he wanted something, he went after it.

"We missed our date at the broker's on Saturday," Luke said when the door closed behind them.

"Good heavens, Luke. Your grandfather had just died. I certainly didn't expect to go shopping for a sailboat."

He set Ellie in the baby carrier and looked about the apartment. He moved to the sofa, shrugged out of his suit jacket, flung it across the back of the sofa then sat down and looked at Lindsay. "I didn't, either. So I rescheduled it. You free this Saturday?"

Lindsay stared at him. He wanted her to go to look at sailboats? Slowly, as if in a daze, she walked to the chair and sat down, placing Ellie between them on the floor. The baby kicked her feet in the carrier and smiled at Luke.

"What about Jeannette?" Lindsay asked.

"What about her?" He leaned back against the cushions and closed his eyes.

"Don't fall asleep," she warned him.

He smiled sadly but kept his eyes shut. "I won't. At least I think I won't. But this is the first peace I've felt since Nurse Spencer woke me up on Saturday morning."

"I know you'll miss him," she said softly.

"For all his faults, he was my grandfather."

"And you loved him."

Luke was silent so long she wondered if he had fallen asleep. Then he spoke. "Yes, I loved him. I've been thinking a lot about when I was a boy and how he taught me things, spent time with me. Took me into the office and proudly showed me what he'd built.''

"He loved you. He also loved being in charge. You're very similar, so I can see why you clashed so much as adults.''

He opened his eyes at that. "I do like being in charge. Does that bother you?''

Shrugging, she tilted her head and stared at him. Why had he stopped by? Was it to do with a divorce? Couldn't he have had his attorneys handle that? She watched him leaning against her sofa, and her heart melted. She wanted to reach out and gather him into her arms and hold him, be held by him.

"Why did you take off so suddenly?'' Luke asked.

Lindsay dropped her gaze to her hands, hoping the tears that felt perilously near wouldn't fill her eyes. She swallowed hard and cleared her throat. "It was time,'' she said.

"My mother has returned to her home. Jonathan's gone. And I thought we were having an affair,'' he said.

She looked up at that. "An affair? For how much longer. Jeannette told me you two had discussed marriage.''

His eyes widened, and he stared at her in surprise. "She said what?''

"She said the two of you had discussed marriage.'' Saying it again didn't make it easier.

"When?''

"Monday, after the funeral.''

"Lindsay, we buried my grandfather on Monday. Do you think I would have discussed marriage with anyone that day?''

"I don't know when you discussed it. Monday is the day Jeannette told me. In the garden, after the funeral.''

"And based on her comments, you pack up and take off?''

"It wasn't exactly taking off, it was coming home.''

"I thought you were home when you lived with me. You

should have given notice on this place and moved out entirely. Damn, a contingency I hadn't expected.''

Lindsay said nothing. There was nothing left to say.

The baby fussed, and Luke looked at her, his expression softening. "How's Ellie been?"

"Fine." The ache caught her unaware. He looked at Ellie with love in his eyes, but he wasn't Ellie's father and would never be.

He settled back in the sofa and closed his eyes again. "God, the office was a madhouse today. I had more calls of condolence than I ever wanted. Some of the old-timers wondered how things would change. I've been running the company for the last year, been fully in charge for the last four months and they still think Jonathan's death would make a major difference. I guess they thought he was still in charge and just letting me play at CEO.''

Ellie fussed again, and Luke reached over to pick her up. She snuggled against his broad chest as one large hand patted her gently on the back. In only a couple of moments she closed her eyes, snuggled close and fell asleep. He leaned back, holding the baby firmly against his chest.

Lindsay felt her heart melt at the picture. She wished she could capture it for all time. Almost holding her breath, Lindsay wondered what to say. He walked in as if he had a right. Settled down on the sofa and began talking about his day. It reminded her of the afternoons during the past few weeks when they'd escape to their room and he'd tell her about his day and ask about hers. Bittersweet memories assailed her. She wanted that forever.

"What did you do today?" he asked lazily.

"Went to the bookstore to see if I could get my old job back," she replied baldly.

Only the slight tightening of his lips gave any indication he'd heard her.

For long moments they sat in silence, then he sighed. "Come home, Lindsay. I miss you."

Her heart leaped at the words. For a blinding moment

hope flared. "What about Jeannette?" she asked.

"The last time I discussed marriage with Jeannette was about six months ago. She accepted my proposal, and then I discovered the manipulations she and my grandfather and mother had schemed. We haven't discussed it since. It's a moot point, I'm already married. Surely you don't think I'd discuss marriage with anyone else while being married to you."

"Maybe not ordinarily, but ours isn't a real marriage."

"Sweetheart, it's about as real as they come. I look forward to coming home every night. To have you and Ellie rush to greet me makes everything worthwhile. I think I handled things badly when Jonathan died, but I hadn't expected to feel the loss so strongly. When I got home yesterday, I wanted things to be as they had been, only you and Ellie weren't there."

"The reason for our marriage no longer existed," she said, wishing she could see his eyes, wishing she had a clue what was going on. Did he mean he wanted them to stay together a bit longer? Or what? "You must have felt it. You…we didn't share a room after your grandfather died."

"The reason we *got* married no longer existed. Does that mean there are no reasons to *remain* married? And I needed a bit of time to myself. I wasn't sleeping and didn't want to keep you awake."

"What do you mean?" Hope built. Only to be dashed down?

Luke rose. "I'll be back in a minute." He carried the baby into her room, laying her gently in the crib, patting her back a minute when she looked as if she might awaken. But she snuggled down. He covered her with a light blanket and turned—almost bumping into Lindsay.

"I couldn't wait. What do you mean?" she asked.

He smiled and drew her into his arms. "I mean, we've weathered some tough times—your dislike and distrust of Balcomb Enterprises and my grandfather, my mother's own charming self."

"Having my life changed by a very demanding man."

"And having an affair with him." Gently he leaned over and kissed her. "I want that affair to continue until we both die," he said softly, kissing her cheeks, her eyelids, her jaw.

"What?" Lindsay knew she was dreaming. Nothing was as it seemed. For a moment she wondered if her longings had overruled common sense. She thought she heard— Her eyes flew open.

"What did you say?"

Luke's dark eyes gazed warmly into hers. "I want our affair to continue until we both die."

He said it loud and clear. She hadn't dreamed it, hadn't imagined the words. Had stared right into his face as he said it.

Stunned, she could only gaze into his beloved face.

"Say yes, Lindsay."

"I thought you loved Jeannette," she blurted.

He shook his head. "I might have thought that at one time, but up against the real thing, it paled."

"The real thing?" Her heart soared. Did Luke love her?

"Yes. You."

"You love me?"

He nodded.

"Me, too. I mean, I love you, too. I can't remember when it happened, but I know one morning I realized you were all I ever wanted. But this whole thing has been so confusing."

His smile blazed across his face before he kissed her long and deep. Lindsay clung, trying to show him with her response how much she loved him. When he scooped her as easily as Ellie, she held on. She would hold on to this man as long as she had breath in her body.

He sat on the sofa, cradling her in his lap. "You haven't said yes."

"Oh, yes, yes, yes! I can't believe it. Do you really love me?" She wasn't dreaming. This was real, wasn't it?

"I really love you, Lindsay. More than mere words can express. I want you in my house when I come home. I want to talk to you about work at the end of each day. I want to watch you raise our children, and I want to take you sailing with me. It'll be an activity that is ours alone."

"I can't believe it. Oh, Luke." She leaned forward and kissed him again. For a long time they were lost to the outside world, dazzled by confessed love.

Some time later, she lay against his chest and smiled softly. She loved him so much and couldn't believe the miracle of his love.

"You have married a demanding man, you know," he said whimsically, playing with her fingers.

She nodded, smiling. So far his demands had matched her own. There was no problem.

"And I'll always run Balcomb Enterprises. But I've made some changes, sweetheart. Safety is a number one priority, far above the bottom line."

"Thank you."

"I'm sorry that Ellie will never know her father, but I'll do my best to be the kind of father you would wish for her. I'm crazy about her, you know that. I would never do anything to hurt her."

"You'll make a wonderful father, Luke. She'll be the luckiest little girl. I thought she would have no one—once we got a divorce."

"If I ever intended to get a divorce, I wouldn't have suggested an affair. But I thought that would be one way to get through to you. I've wanted you since you opened the door to me a few weeks ago. I was grateful to you for marrying me at the time, but so blinded by anger that I couldn't see you. Then when you opened the door, I was bowled over. But you stuck to the terms of the agreement, and I was growing desperate."

"Oh, Luke, I looked awful those last weeks of pregnancy. And I had been so worried. You took care of me, of me and of Ellie, right from the beginning. How could I not love you?''

''I don't want gratitude. God, Lindsay, don't say you feel so grateful you're confusing it with love.'' He pushed her away to stare into her eyes.

''Of course not, silly. I was grateful until you asked for the favor of my pretending to be a loving wife. I felt I was contributing to the deal with that, so the balance shifted a bit. But your patience with your grandfather and mother were a wonder to behold. And your offer of an affair thrilled me. I felt so daring and desirable. And I was already falling in love with you.''

''I don't think you realize how desirable you are. But I'll do my best over the next fifty or sixty years to demonstrate. So, are you ready to come home, now?'' He glanced around the flat. ''Come back with me, sweetheart, and never leave.''

''Your mother may never accept me,'' she said slowly, finding it almost impossible to believe all her dreams were coming true.

''She may never be warmly affectionate, but acceptance will come. Especially with more grandchildren. She's grown quite fond of Ellie. She asked after her yesterday and seemed put out that you were not there. Apparently you helped her on Saturday, and she wants to thank you for that, as well. And it's not as if she'll live with us. She has her own home and circle of friends. Don't make her into an obstacle, Lindsay.''

''I don't want to cause dissension in your family.''

''You are part of that family, and Mother will come around. Jonathan did, you know.''

''What do you mean?''

''He wrote a codicil to his will after all—leaving a tidy sum to you and Ellie. I don't know if he suspected anything at the end, but the wording is clear—he left it to you and Ellie as named individuals, not as relations. He was so crazy about the baby.''

She nodded, remembering the afternoons shared in the sickroom, how he had wanted Ellie to call him Grandpa.

"When she's older, we'll have to show her his picture and teach her to say Grandpa," Lindsay said softly.

Luke cleared his throat. "He would have liked that."

Lindsay jumped up and headed for the bedroom. "I'll begin packing."

Luke followed. "That can wait. We'll send Marabel or Tilly over, and they can take care of that. We'll cancel the lease here and make sure you have no place to run in the future."

She laughed and spun around, throwing herself into his arms. "Luke, I love you so much! I will never want to run anywhere, now that I have your love. Let's go home. And on Saturday, we'll look for that sailboat."

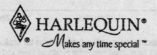

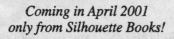

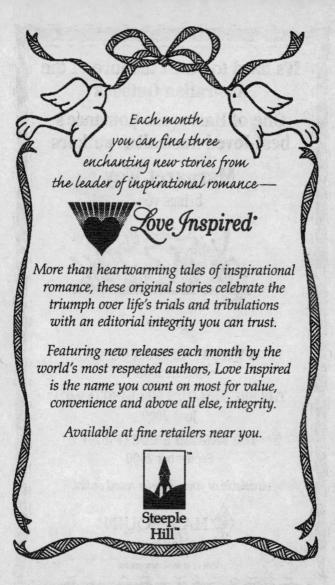